DO NOT REMOVE
CARDS FROM POCKET

The Price of Eggs

SHORT STORIES BY ANNE PANNING

COFFEE HOUSE PRESS : : MINNEAPOLIS : : 1992

The publisher thanks Jerome Foundation; Minnesota State Arts Board; the National Endowment for the Arts, a federal agency; and Northwest Area Foundation for their support of this project.

Coffee House Press books are available to stores through our primary distributor, Consortium Book Sales & Distribution, 287 East Sixth Street, Suite 365, Saint Paul, Minnesota 55101. Our books are also available through all major library distributors and jobbers, and through most small press distributors including Bookpeople, Bookslinger, Inland and Small Press Distribution.

For personal orders, catalogs or other information, write to:
Coffee House Press, 27 N. Fourth St., Minneapolis MN 55401

Library of Congress cataloging-in-publication data
Panning, Anne. 1966-
    The price of eggs / stories by Anne Panning
        p. cm.
    ISBN 0-918273-95-1 : $11.95
    I Title.
PS3566.A577P75 1992
813'.54 – dc20   92-817
                                                         CIP

CONTENTS

This Is Salvation

1

Happy Valentines

7

The Price of Eggs

13

Pigs

37

Insomnia

41

What We Found

57

Rollie Wishes

83

Rudy and Bette's New Year

99

Hired Hand

105

Trailer Court Days

117

for my mother, father, Jim, Amy and Michael
for all the years

This Is Salvation

PENNY

She is a big red-haired girl in her twenties. She struts around the living room, smokes cigarettes, pulls through her hair. She shouts through clenched teeth: I'm going insane! Doesn't anybody want to do anything here? She wants to be insane. She knows a crazy girl who paints and tears it up, paints and tears it up. She thinks that's pretty. She rips her jeans and big white knees poke out, so she's cold.

On Friday afternoons, she buys jugs of three-dollar Chablis and drinks by herself until she gets louder. Rock on, Buddy Holly! she shouts and knocks her knees together. Holds up a fist like a grenade. Saturday mornings she sleeps on a mattress on the floor in Carter Spanky underwear. One leg touches the carpet. She snores until the telephone rings, she says dammit! Wipes her mouth, rubs her eyes but misses by a ring. She turns on the tv, pulls the shades and listens to dusty albums. Asleep again until dark and visitors come knocking. For the fun she is.

JUNIOR

His dad's the drug dealer, and gives to him. This is love. A vcr, leather coat, bag of coke. Two fifties slipped in his pocket besides. But when Junior gives you a bite of his sandwich, he wants one back. To be even. Because of his belly, he eats and eats. To be happy. When he gets unhappy, he rolls on the floor with the remote control. Plays boss with the stations. Changing up and down dizzy. In his bed, he chews the corners of his sheets. Flips through SuperHeroes and always a Coca-Cola.

Without sex, he's irritated. A girl, a guy, I'd screw anything that walks down the street, he tells anyone. So at night, he rubs sugary gel into his hair. Coarse as wool, it fluffs meringue high. He steps out of the house, shoulders back, wide body swinging, Polo smell filling the street. Bootkicking, he'll get one.

MELISSA JANE

She drives the pickup home, a mile out of town. Cassette tapes and pennies on the floor. But a carseat beside her, full of Lucy.

The house peels paint. Empty kegs from old parties clutter the porch. She carries her baby into the house. Sets her keys on the washer. And dryer in the kitchen. Big old dials, speckled insides. Her mother's rejects.

Lucy patters to the half-remodeled living room. Hazy plastic over couch, over open holes. Over the rocking chair from Steven her first Mother's Day. Lucy pulling it off, she shouts no, no! Swings the baby on her hip, thinks of supper in the kitchen. In the cupboards, noodles. Rice.

Canned beans, beets. Oatmeal. In the refrigerator, tupperwares full of tuna salad. Cracked gravy. Curling dry beef.

She calls Steven at the station. Bring something home for supper. Lucy pulls her hair, makes her eyes water. Naughty! she says. Sorting through the mail, bills. Supermarket ads. A letter from her friend Sue. Air mail. She reads it, Lucy on her knee. About Europe, old castles and studying. All that hard work.

JASMINE

She will always smell. Thick minty oils from the co-op. Strawberry incense sticks. Cinnamon breath. Her ears jingle silver baubles. Wrists. Ankles. One day she dyes her bangs white.

Her parents ask her to move because too much tv. She cries, I'm going to tear someone's face off! Forgets her brain pills on the way out. Breaks a big glass of black marbles in the street. It rains.

She lives with a law student because no one else. She has two friends. They smoke together. Everyday pot. Her eyes big walnut cups. Flat Egyptian face. She calls taxis, this way and that.

At night, she sleeps in front of tv. Low murmuring. A guardian angel. White hands blessing her head.

ZACH

Late at night he sets the Mr. Coffee timer. He reels into bed. Always under headphones, his ears flatten. Can't hear. He installs an extension phone right by his bed. Can't hear.

When there is knocking, to the basement. Crumbling cracked cement. Plays the guitar on carpet rolls. Cereal bowl for an ashtray. Camel Lights, Camel straights. When the woman he loves and doesn't calls, he runs to TipTop for groceries. Sausages. Cheese. Real cream for coffee. These are what he remembers from the farm. And the pulse of a hundred milking teats.

His mother calls on Sundays. Has he gone to church? Yes. A rolled-up bulletin to prove it. Is he eating enough? Yes. But a skinny man can't prove it. He hangs up. Shivers. Layers a plaid shirt over his gray sweatshirt. Keeping warm in the city.

CARLYLE

Drives through town in a big lumber truck, waving to everyone. Hair a wooly black mat with sawdust. Tight faded t-shirt, the logo peels off. He builds until lunch. Eats with the married workers at Stu's Rainbow Inn. Large round burgers big as the paper plates. Two pickles. Water-thin malts. He laughs. Gossips out of yellow chipped teeth.

End of the day, he walks home. His parents' home. Still there after so many years. The same route he walked to school.

After supper, he calls Maggie. She won't see him anymore because. You wear out your welcome, she says. He only wants Maggie. He walks uptown to the bar. Ruthie knows, uncaps a bottle of Bud. Cool white smoke slips out like a genie. Around his hot red face. Shot of Cuervo? He nods. White or gold? Oh, gold! he says. He wears the same day's work clothes.

MARLA

She sprawls on the couch, watches tv upside down. Limbs
spread loose like a trashed marionette. Tight homemade
skirt wrinkles around the hips. A show about rape. She
brings her hand to her mouth. Oh! sitting up now, knees
to her chin. Oh! She starts to cry.

But cooking comforts. She splashes Burgundy onto frying meat strips. Stands in front of the stove. Waiting. Arms
crossed over huge sagging breasts. A dingy bustier strains
underneath. She sits alone at the long dining room table. Curls spring
down her back. She twists them. Like pipe cleaners they
stay. The plate cools.

In the bathroom lipstick covers thin flaking lips. Like
wax. Mossy liner around the eyes. Smeared straight out
like cat whiskers. Ready to eat.

SCHMIDTY

He graduated from high school, with D's. Now he's a father
of sorts. To his brothers. Jimmy and Jason don't know any
better. They call their parents at Red Fox Saloon. For arcade
money. What's for supper. He walks the streets with his
mouth open, his cap on.

Baseball brought some fame. He was a poor man's kid,
Schmidty's kid, but could pitch. He made the town team.
Wore spikes from high school that were too small. He liked
driving the bus with the men. Chewing gum, chewing
tobacco. He grew a moustache. Once, his picture in the
paper. He had to cut it out.

But winter backs him up. A down-filled vest is all. Nowhere to go. He sits in the window. Below, women direct
carryout boys with their groceries. His boys in school. Parents at the bar. He wonders how long.

GENEVIEVE

She is from France. French-Indian beautiful, dark. In her small house, only mineral water in the refrigerator. All day she works at the government office. Makes lots of money. She buys records of big bands. She buys colored hose.

Her brother Louie has a shiny tan face. Comes over to interrogate, insinuate. He's wolflike. Long teeth biting. He's been everybody's baby. She loans him money for drinks.

Seldom she sees the rest of her family. Because last Christmas. A sapphire ring she wanted. Her fat mother took jokes. Threw teases. I couldn't afford it, couldn't afford it. But stood in her big Jew house. Big white Cadillac in the garage. Her mother laughed. Threw the small package at her. Smack in the face. Here's your fucking ring. Baby. She left. Her brother and stepfather fistfight.

Now she works hard. Always saving for something.

JIMBOB

Hit by the hockey puck, he went to three doctors. Everybody waited. Now his eye shrinks. Looks up and left. The pupil lopsided. Dull as wax paper.

New York tough. He handles Minnesota winter with a smoke. Big army jacket. Lots of hope. His friends play in bands. Or actors. Long parties. Everyone talks over each other in the kitchen. He breaks out a capsule of cocaine. Not for everyone. They follow him upstairs.

When he visits Hannalynn, brings Dylan Thomas under his coat. Can I read you something? He does. Sort of a love poem. Sort of an elegy. She puts her hands on her knees. That's superior, she says. Read more. He does, for a while.

Happy Valentines

I'M UPSTAIRS sewing cloth hearts onto cardboard. Zigzag around and around and around. I'm Joan, the sick one, don't mind when I throw my lamp against the wall. Lillian's my older sister, way older, forty, and I live with her. She's living with Virgil, this skinny alcoholic. I hate him and he hates me. It works out, except when my medication doesn't work. I sit in my room next to theirs and cry and shriek with laughter back and forth until I throw up. Then I hear Virgil leave the bedroom and the car starts up outside. Fifteen minutes later I hear him crack open a beer and talk quietly with Lillian. She laughs hoarsely. They make it worse. I can't help it, but they do.

It's almost dark. I'm sewing valentines for Lillian and Virgil. Big cardboard ones with yarn ties and watercolors and cloth. I've got a Singer Industrial that I got from the home ec class at the high school. Cheyenne Mountain High School, where I went years ago. I hated that school so much. I was only good at home ec, sewing. Otherwise everyone thought I was pretty dumb, or at least pretty weird. I had two friends, Rona and Darcey. They were both nerds, but everyone thought I was too. I'm chronically depressed, that's all. Nothing I can't handle, except I think I look at most things differently than most people do. That is, I look at most things negatively. It seems everyone in my family wants to be happy, and wants me to be happy. I don't know. It's hard. But if I take my medication, it's all normal at least. And that's the main thing, keeping normal.

I want an Elna sewing machine. Mine's too loud, too big. Elnas are clean and white, hum and float smoothly over fabric. Right now I don't have a job. So I'm on welfare, which really bugs Virgil. I heard him talking to Lillian a few nights ago. "Yeah, sure," he said. "I work all day long so I can support all the crazies in the country. Real fair." I think he's insane. I think he's a red-nosed pervert. Once I was home alone and he came home drunk. I was watching Johnny Carson, and he kept shouting from the bedroom, "Come in here, Joan. Joan, come in here." I turned up the tv as loud as it went and walked nervously around the living room. But I knew. The thought of him lying in that room repulsed me. Crushed red velvet, mirrors with gold veins running through them, the jiggly waterbed. And smells like candy and dirty underwear.

Tonight Lillian and Virgil are taking me out to dinner, Valentine's Day dinner. Lillian's excited. She's been telling me all week, Oh, it's our treat, Joan, it's absolutely our treat. We want to do this. Right now she's at work. She's in charge of the hot lunch program at the elementary school on the west side of Colorado Springs. Every morning she leaves at 6:00 with her hair snug in a hairnet, dressed all in white. I love Lillian. I wish she would leave Virgil. She hangs onto him because she thinks he's got money somewhere, plus she thinks he really loves her. Both untrue as far as I'm concerned. He teaches high school social studies, but he's a drunk. He gets home every night about 9:30.

Lillian runs to the door, ready to love him all up. Most of the time he passes out, though. So Lillian and I sit on the couch and talk about how hard it is to plan a healthy interesting meal for 700 children every day. I tell her not to worry. I tell her not to feel bad. "But I do," she says. "Well, you shouldn't," I say. "You're doing a great job." How do I know if she is or not, but I do that with Lillian, that mothering. She likes it. She curls up her legs on the couch and settles. That's how I know.

I hear keys in the door downstairs. It's Lillian. I can tell by the way she turns them back and forth about three times until it opens. She can never figure it out. I hear two voices, one male, but it isn't Virgil. They rarely come home at the same time. I stop sewing. Lillian's talking. "I'm not sure if she's home or not. Some days she goes for long walks, but I don't know. I'll go check." I push hard on the pedal so she doesn't have to come looking. I wish I wasn't here. I wish I had my own house with my own kitchen and I could cook my own Valentine's Day dinner. I would make huge sugar cookies in the shapes of people I know and paint them with bright red frosting and eat them.

"Joanie, you home? Anybody home?" I hear Lillian climbing the stairs. She has given me this tiny triangle room for sewing. Two windows look out through pine trees. Lillian is heavy, it takes her a long time. She is still wearing her white work outfit. "Oh, you're home, honey, I didn't know." She takes a minute to catch her breath. She's all red.

"I haven't been out today. Is it cold?" I don't know why I ask that. "Are we still going out to eat?"

"Well, depends when Virgil gets home. He's the one that decides this one." She looks at the valentine I'm making, then looks away, like she didn't see it. All for my benefit.

"Joan?"

"What?"

"Oh, nothing. I'll be downstairs. I've got a friend over from work. I'd like you to meet him. He's really nice." She looks at her watch. "What is it, 6:30, not even, so we've got time yet to go out to eat."

I feel like I'm making her nervous. Go ahead and sleep with him, I want to say, but she never would. She should. To hell with Virgil. But I keep sewing, acting like it doesn't phase me that she has a man over. Lillian. I've never seen her talking to any man except Virgil.

"Well, okay then, I'll be downstairs. Come down." I think she wants me to answer somehow. I keep sewing. Lillian moves quickly down the stairs. I stop sewing and look out the window and wonder whether I understand Lillian or not. And does she understand me? Never. She just insists that I live with her to keep us both safe.

By the time it's dark, I have finished one valentine. It is thick and soft in my hands. I smell coffee downstairs and I want to go have some, but Lillian and her friend. Pretty soon it will be too late to go out to dinner. Outside I see Virgil pull up in the pickup across the street. He carries his sweater and tie in his hand. He stops, runs back to the car and unlocks the door. He digs through papers in the backseat and comes out with a bouquet of pink carnations and white roses. He stomps out his cigarette on the wet street.

I start downstairs. Virgil looks surprised to see me standing at the bottom of the stairs ready to greet him.

"What's up?" he says. He looks in the living room. "Where's your sister?" He lights up another cigarette, looks around for an ashtray. "Goddammit," he says and drops ashes on the floor. He rubs them in with his foot. "What are you doing? Where's Lillian? I got her some flowers. Pretty nice, huh?" He holds them up right to my nose. "Hey, this guy doesn't forget Valentine's Day." He's been drinking. I always know because he hardly talks to me otherwise.

"Virgil," I say, "are we still going out to eat tonight?" He smiles and begins to cough.

"It's raining, Joan. Can't you see it's pouring out there?" He stumbles over to the window and taps on the glass with his scrawny hand. "We can't go out in this weather. I could barely drive home."

"I'm sure you couldn't." I walk to the front door and close it, but he doesn't even notice. He's a skinny little mouse I want to kill.

Just then Lillian comes out of the kitchen with her friend who is a very small, gray-haired man. They both hold steaming mugs of coffee. She looks scared. "Hi Virgil," she says and kisses him on the cheek. "This is my friend, Rollie. From work. We were just having some coffee." Rollie holds out his hand. Virgil won't take it. He glares at Lillian.

"Hi, fucking friend. Really great to meet you. I suppose you think you'll be coming out with us tonight for a nice Valentine's Day dinner?" He whacks a big hand on the small, gray-haired man's back. "Well, you're goddamn wrong. I'm taking Lillian out. Maybe you want to take weird Joanie out? She's got no valentine. Right, Joanie?"

I don't answer. Lillian tries to intercept. She takes Virgil's hand and smiles. The small visitor walks slowly to the kitchen and comes back with his coat and hat on. It looks as if he has small tears in his eyes, but I can't decide if it is just the sparkle fading. He looks defeated and sad.

"I'm sorry, Lillian. Good-bye." He tips his hat to all of us and leaves.

"I was just having coffee with him, Virgil. He works with me. Why'd you have to be so rude?" She sits down at one of the dining room chairs, and rubs her eyes.

"Rude? Who's rude? Let's go out to dinner now. All of us. It's Valentine's Day, for chrissake. Oh, shit, I almost forgot. I brought some flowers home for my favorite girl." He picks up the roses and carnations from the floor. He holds the bouquet out to Lillian, then as soon as she reaches for it, he pulls it back and laughs. "Used to be you, Lillian, but now it's Joan." He thrusts the bouquet in my hands and I hold it like a baby that's not mine. Then I throw it back on the floor.

Virgil shakes his head. "Goddamn, I thought the three of us could just go out for a nice dinner. Can't we just do that? Joan, can't you go get ready? And you too, Lillian." Nobody moves.

"I've eaten," I lie. He knows it.

"Just forget it, Virgil. You've already ruined it. Joan and I will just go to McDonald's or something." Lillian starts for the stairs.

"Lillian. Lillian." He catches her before she walks away. "I'm sorry, baby." He pulls her close to him and whispers things I can't hear. He kisses her. "Come on, let's the two of us go out. Come on. Happy Valentine's Day, sweetheart." She leans into his chest. Virgil looks at me until I start walking upstairs. I sit down to my sewing. Lillian laughs and laughs until I hear the door slam and silence. Red lights in the driveway. The Singer Industrial hums in front of me and it's dark and raining hard. I feel bad, only one valentine is done. I have to get a job and get an Elna and make better things.

The Price of Eggs

DANIEL: SUMMER

I can't sleep again. The whole house hangs with a humid stick. Our air conditioner no longer works. It fell from our second-story window last winter and busted. My wife, AnnMarie, sleeps beside me, both arms flung over her head. Her feet hang over the side of the mattress. She looks pained, almost miserable, sweating in her sleep.

In the kitchen I grab a big green tupperware bowl and fill it with cold water. I sit out on the screened porch and sink my feet into the bowl. I don't hear anything but the June bugs whining and screaming through their shells. Then my daughter Erin comes out, thin in her light nightgown. She's sixteen.

"What are you doing up?" she asks.

"I don't know. What are you doing up?" She shrugs her shoulders and sits languidly in the lawn chair beside me. She drinks iced tea. We don't talk for a long time. Whenever it's the two of us, I know what she's thinking. We both know.

"Have you heard anything from Vermont?" She wipes her forehead with her arm. She wants to know about her mother, always, her real mother, Maeve. Erin was only eight years old when Maeve was in the crash right outside of town. But she remembers her, remembers everything.

Now Maeve is a vegetable, I hate calling her that. She stays at Spring Lake Hospital in Burlington, Vermont, the best one. We decided it was for the best that she go far away. Her mother pays the bills; I couldn't. It's almost a thousand dollars a month, but at least she isn't crammed in a room with a dozen schizophrenics watching silly tv. She has her own personal attendant, her own private room. I know all of this from her mother, Georgia. We still keep in touch. She lives across town in a big house by herself.

"I've heard some news, Erin, and I can't believe it. That's why I'm out here thinking."

"Oh," is all she says, almost afraid to know. She longs to have her mother back, but at the same time I think it's her fear. She and my second wife, AnnMarie, get along, but she doesn't call her Mom, she calls her AnnMarie, like some friend. I've been remarried five years. More than that, actually. And now we have the boys, Tony and Ben. I really love AnnMarie, but I can't forget Maeve.

"What do they say?" Erin sticks her toes in my bowl of ice water, splashing.

"I talked to Georgia yesterday on the phone. The hospital called her and said Maeve was improving. She can pick things up, hold a pencil. And she's almost writing letters." The last time I saw Maeve she was in bed, in the hospital here. She had eight broken ribs, a broken leg, a fractured skull, and her skin was all bloated and yellow. But she wasn't there at all, not really. Her chin tilted down to her chest, her eyes gazed dully at her hands. She drooled a silver string that kept breaking.

"I can't believe it." Erin crosses her arms and leans on her knees. She looks hopeful, fired from somewhere behind her dark eyes. "I want to go see her." She leans back, waiting to see what I'll do, to see if there's even a chance. But I don't know what to say. A chill washes over my whole body, despite the heat, and tingles in my head. "Erin, we can't go back to that, you know? This is where we are now. I tell you things about her because I think you should know. But she'll probably never be able to know you, she'll probably never be more than fifth- or sixth-grade level, if that. And that's not a mother or a wife, that's a girl. Erin, don't make it harder than it is."

When I got remarried, I thought this out more than a mind can think. I even prayed, though I'm not religious. I talked to Georgia. I talked to AnnMarie, who was tender and sure. I even talked to Erin about it, who was about twelve then, and she cried and broke our sliding door slamming it so hard. But then we settled. We made a pact. We decided that no matter what happened, Maeve would always be her mother and I would never try to make her think differently. But Erin had her own ideas about love. I tried to explain the different way I loved AnnMarie, never like my love for Maeve, but just as good. But Erin didn't buy it and has been holding it against me ever since.

Erin stands up and stretches her hands above her head, then flops them down. She walks to the screen door and looks out. She's skinny and narrow just like her mother, even her ankles. Her hair is wound up in a knot, but strands hang down her neck, spiraling in the heat. For a second, I want her to go pack, to run upstairs and fill a small suitcase. The Escort sits parked in the street, waiting. We could leave tonight and get there in a day and a half. And AnnMarie would sleep forever. And the boys would play and forget.

"Good night," Erin says and steps into the house before I can say anything.

"Good night," I say back. The June bugs sound desperate for help. I hear a noise back in the house, one of the boys crying, so I go inside. They're sleeping on the fold-out couch in the living room because the window in their room upstairs is painted shut and won't open. A light breeze flies the shades up, then sucks them down again with a clap. But it's a hot breeze, almost worse than no breeze. Tony sits up in the bed, sheets pulled up to his mouth.

"Tony, what's the matter?" He sniffles, gasps for air in short jerks. He rubs his eyes with the sheets. "What's the matter, huh?"

"I can't sleep with such hot," he says, shaking his head. Ben sleeps next to him, curled tight under the pink sheet. His bangs are soaking wet.

"Come here." I pick Tony up in my arms. His sticky body sucks to my bare chest. I carry him outside and stand him in the bowl of water. "How do you like that?"

"Mmm-hmm," he says, marching up and down.

ERIN'S PICTURE

Above my bed, the three of us in tarnished frame. My real mother, Maeve. We stand laughing by Popeye's Chicken in Chicago. My mother is young. She hugs the bucket like a belly. Her white t-shirt ripples in the wind. Long hair in her mouth, her eyes, blowing in my father's face.

He wears a Dodgers cap. He smells her. They share secrets. I stand on the patio table, swinging Mom's hand. I squint at her. My father looks too. Says she is alive. Cries she is full of honey and days.

ANNMARIE: INTRODUCTIONS

I'm originally from Pittsburgh, but my work brought me here to Minnesota. I'm director of the St. Mary's Good Samaritan Center, the only nursing home in Walcott, which is a pretty small town. Everyone around here really *is* a good samaritan. People I didn't even know welcomed me in like I was their best friend. It was uncomfortable, actually. Women in my neighborhood brought over pans of bars. Couples offered me their telephones or cars if I had any trouble. I kept my distance, for a while. Then I realized, like everywhere else, they're just people. Now I really like it here, but that's a long and confusing story in itself.

I was in the K-Mart one Saturday looking around in the shampoos and soaps, and so was this man I had never seen before. He looked puzzled, absolutely lost, so I asked him if I could help him with anything. He said he felt stupid, but his twelve-year-old daughter just started her period and he didn't exactly know what to buy for her. I thought he was charming, standing there scratching his head. I wondered about his wife, if he had one, or if he was divorced or just being an interested father. I scanned some shelves and put a small pink box in his cart. That should be the right thing, I said. Thanks a lot, he said, then seeing my purse in my cart and my list, he slapped his hand up to his forehead. I'm sorry, he apologized, I thought you worked here. You know, that smock you're wearing . . . how could I be so stupid? Oh, don't worry about it, I said laughing, it's perfectly okay. The smock's from work. Oh, really, where do you work? he asked, his blush fading. I'm director of the nursing home, the Good Samaritan Center? I'm new. Oh, really, yeah, my father was in there for a while a few years back until he died. He was real sick.

We both fell silent and then he said thanks again, and wheeled off. I had to laugh, him thinking I worked there. I took the smock off and threw it in my cart.

A few weeks later I was roaming around Red Owl, trying to find something for supper. It's hard cooking for only one person. A big full-course meal doesn't seem worth it. I was looking in the cheese cooler when I spotted him again and realized I didn't know his name. He and his daughter were lifting up squares of wrapped hamburger. He kept throwing packages back and forth between his hands like footballs, which seemed to annoy his daughter. She took the biggest brick of meat, pointed out the price and poundage, and threw it in their cart. He laughed. Then, as he turned around looking for a new direction, our eyes met. I quickly looked away, then smiled. We wheeled our carts next to each other and said hello.

"We just keep running into each other," he said.

"I know," I said, laughing. I felt uncomfortable. The daughter stared me up and down with her black eyes. She was skinny and wore a long brown braid.

"Oh, I'm sorry, this is my daughter, Erin. She's having a slumber party tonight and we're trying to throw together some sort of barbecue feast." He slapped the hamburger brick in the cart. His daughter looked so pissed off I thought she was going to hit him. He nudged her.

"How do you do?" she held out her hand and I shook it. Again there was an awkward silence, until I finally said, "Well, I'm just trying to find a little supper here myself. So, I better get going." I told Erin it was nice meeting her and asked him his name.

"Oh, I'm sorry. Daniel. Daniel Wells. I teach science up at the high school." I shook his hand.

"Oh, really? Great. I'm AnnMarie Franz. Have a good slumber party," I called to Erin, who was already digging in the next aisle.

"Thanks," she said unenthusiastically. He wheeled away and I wheeled away, but there was something strange exchanged between us. I was definitely attracted to him. He was good-looking and friendly and interesting, but there was also a hollow distance, a mystery that caught me. I was surprised when he called me a week later. He rambled, apologized, explained, and the whole time my heart was frenetic. My hands were clammy on the phone and my breathing was short. I hadn't felt that way in years. And I could tell it was difficult for him too, but he finally did it, asked me out to dinner.

"Do you like Mexican or Chinese? And don't say you don't care." He had a clear voice like blue sky, but there was still a ring of pain behind it.

"I like both, but Mexican would be great." After we hung up, I sat there like a teenager and thought, without moving, how this would go. Would he tell his daughter? Obviously, he wasn't married. But then I realized how little I knew about him.

I hadn't been involved with anyone since Gomez Pineda, a Spanish-Mexican illegal alien who lived with me and wanted to marry me. I never did, thank god, but we lived together in a garage apartment for two years. I think I almost loved him, but then I realized he would never love me back the way I wanted him to because he wanted citizenship more than he wanted me. He said that wasn't true, but I don't know. Finally, he figured I wasn't going to go along with his plan, so he took off, which was fine with me.

So I was single, in my thirties, and felt ready for a relationship when I met Daniel. Not that I was out looking, but the timing was right. I was able to be honest with Daniel. And he was honest with me. Although I could never have guessed the stories he had to tell, the things he relived every day of his life.

SECOND WEDDING

Everybody sits in pews tight. The daughter stands in a long pink gown with a ring of roses in her hair. Her father wears a gray suit, plain and simple. The new wife moves through ivory, tiny pearls caught around her neck like teeth. The diamond ring he twists around her finger is ruby. She turns into it. Nobody claps. The old grandmother reads two Shakespeare sonnets, and the man and woman drink from a large silver cup. She shivers. He sucks the wine between his teeth. The girl's roses start to prick her head. Tiny wet scratches on her scalp. No one sees her eyes watering. They are busy looking straight ahead at the cross, their salvation. After the kiss, Pastor disappears through the side door. Big pink bows sag into the aisles.

HOW MAEVE FLEW

It is a gorgeous day, the day before Easter. I drive our van around, doing some errands. I pick up an Easter lily for my mother at the florist, buy bags of malted milk balls and marshmallow bunnies and, of course, jelly beans for Erin's Easter basket, and as I'm about to turn into our driveway, I remember the eggs. Erin reminded me before I left to pick some up, the biggest and best eggs for dying tomorrow at Grandma Georgia's. But I don't like the eggs they sell in the grocery stores. They aren't fresh and they're such puny things I just can't see paying almost a dollar a dozen. And Erin wants to dye lots of Easter eggs.

So I turn off onto the highway and head out to my friend Clara Norman's. I used to work with her at the hospital, and she told me, anytime, to come out and get some eggs. She has a small farm full of chickens running every which way, squawking at your legs when you walk up to the front doorstep. I turn off about a mile later to the gravel road that leads to her driveway. Everything is absolutely golden. I turn into Clara's driveway, and sure enough, a dozen or more chickens come flapping and scrambling at my van. Clara steps out on the front doorstep, shielding her eyes from the glare. Then she waves and comes down to greet me.

"Maeve! How are you?" She hugs me and pats me on the back. "What brings you out this way?" She stands looking at me with one foot slightly in front of the other and smiles.

"I came to see if I could get some eggs. Do you have any? Erin wants to dye eggs tomorrow."

"What kind of question is that? Course I have eggs. Let me go and get you some kind of container." She hurries off to the house and I wait, watching the sun sink down in the west. In a minute she comes out carrying a huge round basket with a freshly pressed dishtowel in the bottom.

"Keep this, Maeve. My Easter present." She laughs and leads me out to the barn. In a huge straw-lined bin are plenty of eggs. "Take what you like, then come on in for some coffee." She leaves me with the shrieking chickens as I carefully pick up eggs, placing the biggest ones softly in the basket. When I have over three dozen, I call through Clara's screen door.

"I have to go back home, Clara. I have to fix some supper. How much for the eggs?" I dig around in my purse for some loose bills.

"Oh, you just forget about that," she says, waving her hand. We talk through the screen door briefly, then I tell her I really have to go.

"Won't you just have one cup of coffee?" She's a widow and seems lonely. "The sun hasn't even gone down yet."

"I'd love to, Clara, but I really have to go. See you soon."
I head out to the van, chickens scampering around my feet
so I can barely walk without tripping. Out on the road,
shadows collect and one side of the road is dark. The sun
glows copper all over the fields. I roll down my window.
I put the basket of eggs on the seat beside me, the seat belt
fastened around them in case I have to stop suddenly. Back
on the main highway, the glare is terrific. I breathe in all
the fresh air. Erin will probably be waiting at the door. I
left the roast in the sink to thaw. Hopefully Daniel is starting dinner.

As I look right to check for cars at the intersection, I feel
the blow first like a gust of wind, then sharp, like frayed
metal. My head turns slow motion and sees the red pickup.
Its silver snout rips open my door, my body. Then the van's
stick shift stabs through my leg like a big needle. All wetness on my face. Cold streaming wetness, covering my
eyes to black. Then I can only feel. My stomach balloons
into my ribs, my fingernails break off with the force, my
vertebrae crackle, fizz like carbonation.

From then on, my head foams bubbles. Someone stirs
with a fork and knife, pours gasoline, alcohol, flames,
mountains into it. Tiny silver needles prick my face. I land
softly on the sod with a pat.

And the strangest thing that bothers me, I see you get out
of the truck, but you don't look into the van. You don't even
notice that all Erin's Easter eggs are smashed, yellow yolk
splattered on the windows. Tiny pieces of jagged shell,
white flakes drifting all over the seats.

Then my mind snaps like elastic wire and cools.

ERIN'S EASTER WISH

It is Easter Day. We are at Grandma Georgia's. The sun is gigantic and bright white on the linoleum floor. Grandma Georgia is smiling, standing in her pastel plaid housedress. Square crinkled face, wide box hips, round wire glasses. She sets one hand on my mother's shoulder. My mother touches it, rubs the dusty hand with her soft one.

A huge kettle boils dozens of eggs. On the table, white porcelain teacups steam full of hot water and vinegar. All in a row. My mother hands me each tiny pellet, and I drop one in each cup. Cardinal red blooms up from the bottom. Indigo blue. Yellow like warm urine. Fast jade green. And rose like winter cheeks, cotton candy syrup. Every time I drop in a pellet, I look back at my mother and she says, Oh look at that, with wide eyes. Grandma Georgia spreads a bath towel on the table, rolls the boiled eggs dry. My mother bends three spoons and hands me one. Grandma Georgia wraps a dishtowel around me tight. Careful not to stain that pretty dress, she says, and ties me in back. I hold an egg in my hand. The warmth spreads from inside and I hold it to my cheek. I hold it to my mother's cheek. She closes her eyes and smiles. I believe I have made her that happy.

With a stubby white crayon, she prints on the white bone egg. I can't see what she is writing. Grandma Georgia draws long squiggles and waves and circles with her crayon. I keep mine plain. I watch my mother as she dips the spooned egg into the rose teacup, the other half in jade. She blows on it, sets it on newspaper. What is it, what is it? I say, jumping up and down. She holds it up by her face and says, read. I LOVE MY BABY, I read. Me! I shout, pounding on my chest. That's right, she says.

Only you're no baby anymore, Grandma Georgia says, and starts whistling. I let my eggs sit in the cups for a long time, longer than my mother or Grandma Georgia. Because I want my eggs to be dark and rich like jewels.

I know, says Grandma Georgia, raising up her palms, let me take a picture! She wipes her hands on her apron and shuffles to the next room. She holds a clunky black Polaroid and shouts Act natural! So my mother and I keep dunking eggs and looking at each other. We don't talk anymore because of the camera. Take it, Grandma Georgia, I say. I can't see the two of you, she says. Scoot over, Erin, on the other side of the table.

So instead, I stretch my whole body and twist myself over by my mother. Still can't see you, Grandma Georgia says, move over. And by that time I'm practically laying on top of the table and just as she shouts, Smile, I feel warm water on my knees and dress. Grandma Georgia rips out the instant picture she took. We all three watch the dyes mix into one brown color and drip onto the floor in steady streams.

Get something to wipe it, Grandma Georgia says, not angry. But I feel terrible. Three of the colors are gone. I sit down on the kitchen chair as my mother wipes up with a damp rag.

It's all right, Erin, my mother says, wringing brown into the sink.

Sure, Erin, everybody spills, Grandma Georgia says. And they sit back down and start dipping the rest of the eggs into blue and green. I wait for the picture to develop in front of my eyes, but Grandma Georgia must not have done it right because it stays black.

DANIEL: DRIVING

I never do sleep. It happens a lot. After the cooling water, Tony finally falls asleep in my lap. I carry him back to the house, lay him down next to his brother. I find a little fan in the kitchen and set it up on the table in front of them. The quick breeze makes Ben quiver in his sleep, itch his nose and roll over, covering Tony with his arm.

I sit in the kitchen with a pitcher of iced tea in front of me. AnnMarie has left files of some of her residents on the table, so I read through them. Melva has glaucoma and prefers to use the lavatory by herself. She is allergic to milk and other dairy products and cannot have caffeine. Melva is extremely temperamental and will try to con workers as well as fellow residents to get her way. After reading through all of them, I push the files away. Outside, two squirrels chase each other around a tree. It's almost light out.

I hear AnnMarie moving around upstairs. The house is so old, everything creaks. Most summer mornings she's up early. I know what she'll ask me, too. Where was I all night? What was I doing? I don't expect her to understand. Some nights I'm practically pulled out of bed, led downstairs, outside, to wait for something. It isn't always Maeve. It's more than that.

"Good morning," I feel AnnMarie's arms around my neck from behind. Her hands are cool and smooth. "Couldn't sleep, huh?" She sits at the chair opposite me and starts pulling on socks. She's wearing a t-shirt and shorts so I assume she's going running. "Want to come with me?" she asks, lacing up her shoes. "I'm only going two miles because it's so hot. But I figure I better go before it gets too hot. What's in there?" she asks, looking into the orange pitcher.

"Was iced tea, but it's gone. Sorry."

"Oh, that's okay. Are the kids still sleeping?"

"Yeah, they are, I think." I don't tell her about Tony waking last night, it doesn't seem important. I go to the sink and run cold water over my wrists.

"So, do you want to come with me?" She leans on the counter next to me, winding her hair up in a binder. "Come on."

"No, I think I'll pass. I just can't. I might take the kids for a drive when they wake up. Get some ice cream or something. But I'll see you later." I take her face in my hands and look into her eyes. Then something scares me about us, standing in the kitchen. I hold her close to me and tell her I love her. I need to tell her that before she goes. She smiles and the screen door slams behind her.

I go back out to the screened porch. It's been over seven years now and I keep thinking about Maeve. Not always, but certain days, certain feelings in the weather and sky. I'm not unhappy now, with the boys and AnnMarie, but Erin understands. We still share the strange bond. Erin won't forget. She cooperates with AnnMarie and I think she may even love her in her own way, but she's looking for Maeve, always. Maybe it would have been easier if she had died.

I hear space guns shooting, then the sound of commercials. The boys are up, watching tv. For some reason I'm excited to see them. They sit up in the couch-bed in their white underwear. Both have blond hair—that's AnnMarie. Tony waves to me with his blanket in his hand.

"We're watching cartoons," he says. His eyes light up.

"I know," I say, sitting down at the end of the bed. "Want to go for a ride?" Ben doesn't hear me. He's too absorbed by the action on tv. The room is dark and the tv shines watery off his eyes.

"I do," shouts Tony, jumping on the bed. "Where will we go?"

"Anywhere we want," I say. "Go put some shorts on and we'll go." He runs off, bare feet slapping the wooden floor. "Where's Mom?" Ben asks. He's four years old and thinks he's about twelve. We don't get along lately. For some reason, Ben feels an animosity toward me and I don't know why. The boys don't know anything about Maeve. AnnMarie and I decided it wasn't important to tell them until they were older. I felt that was AnnMarie's right. They're her children, our children.

"I'm not coming. I want to watch cartoons." Ben turns up the sound and crosses his arms.

"Why don't you come with us? Mom's gone, I can't leave you here alone." Actually, Erin's home, but I don't tell him that. He glares at me, then stomps out of the room.

The boys and I climb into the Escort, careful not to put our legs down too fast on the burning seats. Ben sits in back. He rolls his eyes as I fasten his seat belt. Tony sits in front with me, his seat belt snapping wide across his chest. No air conditioning in the car either, so we open all four windows. I don't know where we're going. Sometimes I just like to get out of town. I pull out onto Highway 10. The Circle Cafe is this way and we can get ice cream cones there.

As we're driving, we pass the intersection near Clara Norman's where Maeve was hit. I don't try to drive out here on purpose, but I bring myself out here all the time. I drive slowly, watching the stream run through the ditch. Litter and tractor tires line the bottom. The boys look down from their windows, expecting an animal or something. There's nothing.

"Why you driving so slow?" Tony asks, still looking out the window. "Did you see a skunk?" We were reading about skunks the other day, and I told him there were plenty of them around, you just had to keep your eyes open.

"No, I was just looking. It's such a nice day." I catch Ben's glare in the rearview mirror. He doesn't buy anything I say these days. I speed up, crossing over train tracks and speed bumps.

"Where we going?" Ben whines. "I'm hot." Tony turns in his seat to look back at him. He follows Ben's cue, sinking back into his own seat.

"Yeah, I'm hot." Then he looks back to see what's next. Ben pouts.

"You two aren't any fun." Actually, I want to shake Ben sometimes. He's an ornery kid, and he gets Tony acting the same way. Ben's four and Tony's three, so naturally Tony'll do anything Ben does.

I press on the brake. "Do you want to go home, or do you want to get some ice cream?" Neither of them answer at first. Tony looks back at Ben.

"We want ice cream," Tony decides. Ben waits for us in the parking lot. Tony carries a peppermint bonbon, dripping, to him. "Here you go," he says, licking at the melting sides.

"Don't lick it!" Ben says, "I don't want it after he licked on it." He gets back in the car. I take the cone in my hand and hold it to his window.

"Do you want this or not?" Ben shakes his head. "Fine. I guess Tony and I'll have to eat it." I start licking it. I hate stooping to his level, but he gets me so angry. As we pull out of the parking lot, I throw the cone out the window. I don't want it. And Tony's having enough trouble with his own, dribbling green all over his bare stomach and onto the seat. I swing the car around with one hand, and drive back to town another way. Maeve would love Tony, I just know it.

MAEVE: WHEN I THINK ABOUT

pieces of glass   folding under my skin   horn in my head
daddy mamma   swinging me an underdog at Beavey
Park   July Dottie dog biting my leg and crying   slides
standing over heat vent in flowered nightgown   blowing
up   fat flannel   and hot legs
    kewpie doll necklace in fourth grade   chairman of win-
dowsill committee   decorating old radiator with sticky
tape   withered bleeding crepe paper   nobody looks
huckleberry finn   daddy loud   with brown hearing
piece in his ear   pick it out   take it out   can't hear you
    fat patties i fry in mud   mamma give a big pan to cook
big leaves in puddle water for soup   nancy never shares
she pull out ribbons from braids   soak them in more puddle water   grandma throw them in soap   nancy keep
mean nancy never let me play on her side
    split bones and bloody swallowing   thick dull plastic
over eyes   staring   onto white sheets   big woman lifts
me up   holds me over toilet   crouches   kleenex wiping
down again over side   small square window   the door
big   small growing   thick pencils   in my fingers   live
water sounds in my ears   calling out   forward from
inside   let me   let me   freezing in the box   long arms
call up   let me whisper   scream

DANIEL: THAT ALMOST EASTER

Erin is in the tub. I hear her singing, then making car
sounds. A week ago she turned eight years old. We had a
party — Maeve, Georgia and I — and we had fun. We bought
her a lavender bike with a white banana seat. Her grandma
bought her two Barbie dolls, probably her last year for that,

that's what Georgia figures. Erin has the dolls with her in the tub. I hear her making them talk like they are in a beauty shop, washing their hair for a price. I laugh.

It's past dark and Maeve isn't home yet. No sign of the van. The roast in the sink is thawed and watery. There is no note. I'm not even sure I know how to make a roast, so I get out a big casserole pan and a frying pan. If I remember right, you're supposed to brown meat in a frying pan, then put it in a casserole with water and cook it. So I do this. The roast is ice cold and bleeds all over my hands. One side turns a dull gray, so I flip it over with a fork. Sprinkle salt and pepper. It smells like a burger, looks like a pork rear.

As I'm pouring water into the casserole, the phone rings, and somebody knocks at the door. It's probably Maeve with her arms full, so I let the phone ring and answer the door. It's not Maeve. It's Ray Wagner, a policeman I know. I let him in.

"Mommy?" Erin calls from the tub.

"No, Erin, it's not Mommy. She's not home yet." I tell Ray to sit down at the table, that I'm making dinner, and by that time the phone has stopped ringing. He doesn't sit down.

"I came to tell you about your wife. She's been in an accident just north of town. You better come up to the hospital right away." He touches his hat, then his belt.

"Maeve?" I ask. He nods. "What do you mean?"

"Daddy, I want to get out," Erin hollers from the bathroom.

"I have to get my daughter out of the tub," I tell him. "She'll get cold if I just leave her in there."

He nods again. I stop on my way to the bathroom. "Will you help me?" He takes me by the shoulders and sets me down in a dining room chair. Erin keeps splashing.

"Can I call anyone?" Ray asks me. "Anyone who can look after your daughter?"

"Call Georgia."

"Georgia . . . ?"

"Georgia, her grandma. Maeve's mother. Georgia Byers. Call her."

While he is on the phone, I go off to the bathroom and wrap a huge yellow towel around Erin and lift her out of the tub. Her small fingers are wrinkled and old. "I've got to go somewhere, honey. Grandma Georgia is coming over." She puts one hand on my shoulder for support while I rub her dry.

"Where's Mommy?" She lifts up her arms as I pull the nightgown over her head. Her face pops through. "Huh?"

"She got sick and had to go to the hospital. I'm going to see her. I'll come and get you later." Before Erin can ask a thousand questions, I carry her into the living room and start talking to Ray. Within minutes, Georgia appears, gray hair wound in rollers.

"I came as fast as I could," she says, short of breath.

"I'll call you," I say. Maeve's her daughter, I think, looking back at mine with wet hair and bath cheeks.

At the hospital, they roll Maeve off the elevator, all wrapped in white. Red stains around her head, her legs. I think of the meat at home, runny in my hands. I don't know where to go, who to follow. In a large room full of silver, they uncover her. I step back, and inhale. I didn't expect all the black. Black blood. Dirt, gravel. Puffed eyelids. Nothing straight, everything cracked with black.

They ask me to leave for a while. I do what they say. Maeve isn't pretty anymore. I can't remember how old she is.

In a few hours, they know Maeve is not going to be paralyzed. A broken leg, broken ribs, and something they don't know with her head. Her heart is steady, so she won't die. In a few hours, after about five specialists have arrived, they know something more, from a CAT scan. A certain part of her brain was pulverized. This means, said Dr. McCarver from Mayo Clinic, that she may be a vegetable. "I have to call Georgia," I say. "I have to get my baby." Everyone looks at me, worried. "I'm okay." I sit down in the chair and try to remember my phone number. "I can't remember my phone number!"

"It's all right," I hear Maeve say. I start looking around for her. Then they get me settled with a white pill.

And hours, days, months, years later, who knows, we decide to send Maeve off to Burlington in Vermont, to the best hospital. There is nothing else to do. After practically living at the hospital, we cry, Erin and I, as we say good-bye. But Maeve doesn't look at us. She stares at the floor, always.

"I'm sorry, Maeve," is the last thing I tell her.

And after three years, I realize finally, that I will never have Maeve again. That she can't be my wife. Or Erin's mother. Finally, I divorce Maeve. As much as I'd rather have myself slaughtered, I sign the papers and let her go.

ANNMARIE: ABOUT VERMONT

I come back from my run and the house is empty and quiet. The car is gone. The empty pitcher sits on the table where Daniel left it. It's already 85° and it's not even noon. My whole body is red from the heat, so I go to the bathroom to start a cool shower. The door is closed. It must be Erin, looking at her skin in the mirror or curling her hair to have it fall out again in the humidity. Maybe she's bathing. She's forever bathing.

I don't have the energy to climb the stairs to the other bathroom, so I wait in the kitchen. I pour myself some milk and put dishes in the dishwasher. The bathroom door opens and Erin walks into the kitchen, hair falling clean and straight down her back. We've become friends, finally, but it isn't always easy. She resents me in a way. She truly believes her mother will get better. Miracles like that don't just happen that often, that's what I think.

"Will you French braid my hair?" She sits down at the table and shakes her head. I was going to take a shower, but this seems more important now. Daniel always says that Erin tries reaching out to me, but I just don't realize it. This may be one of those times. And even though I'm exhausted and hot, I say I'll do it. She runs to the bathroom and gets a long thin comb. I part her hair and tell her to hold on to one side. She hums. I hold sections of her hair like animal tails in my fingers.

"AnnMarie?" She half-turns her head and I move with her.

"Umm-hmm?"

"I need to talk to you about something." She has taken to calling me by my first name, which I guess I don't mind. I don't try to be her mother. I don't ask her to treat me like I am. But it feels odd, her calling me AnnMarie and the boys always hollering Mommy.

"What is it?" I have a hard time starting the braids. Her hair is so clean and shiny, it slips.

"Well, I was talking to Dad last night. It's just an idea. It's about Vermont. Don't take any of this against you, but I want to go out there. I heard my mom is getting a little better and I want to see her."

I don't know what to say. "What did your dad say?"

"He told me to forget it. But, see, I don't want to. Grandma Georgia said she'd take me out there this summer if I wanted to go. What do you think?"

I fasten a binder around one braid and think for a minute before starting the next one. I can understand wanting to see her mother, but this is so complicated. She's a vegetable. It might be harder than Erin realizes.

"She still won't know you, you know. But this is up to you. I'll talk to your father about it, to see how he feels. Erin, I understand, but this is a hard one." The second braid is almost finished. They go down past her shoulder blades. Maeve had long, long hair, from pictures I've seen. I think that's why Erin keeps hers long. She wants to be just like her mother, hold on to all she can. It scares me in a way, the thought of her and Georgia going out there, Maeve getting better and better. Because the news would reach Daniel, and what then? How would that be? Although I just can't see it happening.

ERIN: WHAT YOU DO

You go to the airport with two blue bags in your hands. Georgia carries a big red one, full of both your clothes and some cookies. Inside your smallest bag, you carry a cloth book, colored pencils and a hairbrush. You keep the bags closed.

Georgia snores and drops the newspaper. You pick it up and press it to your knees. The airplane scales up and up. The flight attendant brings you clear pop in a cup. Your stomach falls flat. You drink it fast and suck the ice. Georgia wants out of her seat belt. But the light's on.

You follow everyone off. The air is fresh near the door. Then everyone frightens you. The flight attendants who say, Bye-bye now. The hand-held children. Men with video cameras, women under hats. Georgia pulls you close. So this is Burlington, she says. As you ride in the back seat, a Vermont summer feels different. Fewer sprinklers, smaller houses. The cabbie plays music you like. Georgia puffs, too much moving. The rearview mirror is angled to you, so you keep looking. Messy blowaway hair. Tip him, you tell Grandma Georgia after it is too late. From the fourth-floor hotel window you see small hills and a blue river. You sit in the bathroom for a long time. Your back to the mirror. That night you sleep with your feet palmed against Georgia's. The dreams creak like old stairs. Everyone plays fingers with your hair.

In the morning, you brush. Georgia clicks her teeth, locks the door. Your father's voice echoes in your ears. He wants to come along. Never say that, he says. Never go. But there is your mother's door with the small window. You wish you were that small. Could stand inside the square and peek inside with miniature hands. Georgia nods. Swings open to Maeve. Sitting on the unmade bed.

You see your mother. Forget the flowers and Easter. Nothing repulsive. Her hair is clipped blunt to the chin. She lives. Only to keep track of her hands, picking the sheets. Feeling the back ties of her gown. Her toes waver. You want to rub them, but you don't.

Georgia picks up. You watch carefully how she touches her. Like a small girl. Each time, your mother's head bobs like water. Crazy cow eyes dipping along. When she speaks, you shudder. Long wet vowels. Hold your arms with a chill. You don't understand, so you leave. You drag yourself to a place that's bigger. To the sidewalk. And lean against the building.

HOME

Tonight Daniel watches AnnMarie cut open watermelon and lay wedges on paper plates. The boys pick out seeds before biting. This is about 9:30 when summer starts darkening. She will not look into his eyes.

Erin is gone. Her absence carves a black hole they might fall into. Each word is carefully tuned. He thinks about saying, I will never leave you. But doesn't.

They sit outside at the picnic table with their shoes thrown underneath. Sometimes somebody waves from a car, a student of Daniel's or a friend. Tony holds up his plate for more, but spills the juice from the last. It runs through the cracks of the table, dribbling onto Ben's bare feet. He jumps back, bitter, and stomps to the house. The porchlight goes on. AnnMarie sighs. She gives Tony another piece and herself one too.

When the crickets start chirping and the mosquitoes bite, it is over. They stand up and throw juice off the plates into the grass. Daniel wants to take AnnMarie in his arms, but can't. She is too busy.

Pigs

"IVAN WILLIAM," Olive hollered at the house, "you get down here and help your mother. The damn pigs are loose." Ivan was her only son, her only child. Every day he fed the pigs and splashed fresh water in their trough. "What's wrong, Mom?" He stood in red pajamas on the cement steps, a hand covering his eyes from the early morning sun.

"What do you mean, what's wrong? The pigs broke out of that damn fence I've been asking you to fix for the past three weeks. Now, get moving." She wiped her dirty hands on her dress and spat in the gravel.

Ivan rubbed sleep from his eyes. He was the man of the house now, and he hated that. His father had left when Ivan was in kindergarten. Just like that. Mom had sent him into town to pick up some milk and buns, and he never came back. People said he ran off with a young girl, Renee, the librarian. Ivan didn't know what to believe, only it felt as if his father was dead and now he had to run the entire pig farm at the age of twelve.

Ivan ran up to his room and dressed. It was so hot he didn't need a shirt. In the mirror his chest caved in, bony and smooth. He straightened, pulling back his shoulders. From the window, he saw his mom running around the pigpen, shit smeared all over her legs. She waved a broom at the pigs and tried to get them back into place. Instead, they wandered to the house, tearing up the green lawn to black. His mom raised her hands to the sky and shook her head.

Ivan felt a sinking in his stomach. He worried that she really was crazy, the way people said. When he got his haircut at Hal's last week, he overheard some men talking as he left. "Yeah, the poor kid. Olive really lost it when Cliff left her, that's for sure. She's crazy as they come."

Ivan had begun watching his mom closely. After supper last night, he found her stuffing chewed-up corn cobs into cupboards, dirtying clean dishes. "Why are you doing that?" he asked her. She whirled around with wide eyes and hugged him hard. Then she sat on the floor and cried.

Now Ivan ran outside and picked up a thick oak branch from the ground. Damn pigs! He saw his mother stooped over in the mud. He ran up behind her, and there was his new pig, Chiz, bleeding and limp. His mom held it close to her chest, bloodying her dress and arms.

"Goddamn swine. They stomped right over her, and now she's hurt." She petted the coarse hair, smearing red into it. "Look at what happened, Ivan. You just stand there. Help me."

"What should I do?"

"What should you do? What should you do? Help me, Ivan." She sobbed and rocked back and forth with the dead pig. Chiz had been his favorite, named after his best friend, Tom Chizmadia. Now its stomach was torn, and its head was blue and purple and red.

"Ivan, go get the keys to the pickup from the kitchen counter. Go now."

"But—"

"Get them!" she hollered, flopping the pig's head to one side as she turned.

He found the keys and returned, standing beside her, out of breath.

"Now get the truck started. Let's get this pig some help."

"Mom, I can't drive. I'm not old enough."

"You're old enough if I say so. Now get going."

"No, I'm not. I don't want to. I can't." He felt like crying.

"Then you're no son of mine, Ivan William Klaybur." She whispered his name right up to his face and dropped the pig in the mud. "Now pick up that pig and bring it over to the truck."

His mom hobbled over to the truck. She had never had a driver's license. He heard the motor start and gravel crunch under the tires. She pulled up next to him. Dust from the road blew in his eyes.

"Get in here before the damn thing dies. That's all we need."

"But it's dead, Mom. Look, it's not even breathing."

"That doesn't mean anything. Let's go now."

He picked up the dead pig. It was heavy and reeked of shit and sour innards. Yellow juice was trailing out of its gut. His mom swung open the door, and he climbed in. The truck was intolerably hot from being shut up. He laid the pig over his bare legs. Its mouth was open and blood drooled out. His mom's small hands gripped the steering wheel tightly.

They bounced down the narrow driveway, and looking back, he saw the loose pigs watching them drive away. They seemed sad and apologetic to Ivan, as if they hadn't meant to cause any trouble. His mom stared straight ahead, biting her lips, sweating. He let the wheat fields fade past in a blur.

When they slowed into town, he saw his friends Ron and Steve, buying pop from the Pepsi machine at the gas station. He looked down at the pig on his lap, heavy and wet. His mom drove down Main Street past the barber shop and both grocery stores. Ivan wondered if she would stop at the doctor's office or the animal clinic. She kept driving.

When they reached the blacktop highway, Ivan was worried. The blood from the pig was drying sticky on his legs.

"Mom, where are we going?"

She didn't answer right away, just lit a cigarette and flicked ashes out the window. "We're going to find your father. He's the only one who knows how to take care of these damn pigs, and he's going to do it."

Ivan swallowed. The pig was crusted and brown from the air of the open window. Ivan laid it gently on the floor by his feet, half-expecting a protest from his mom. He stuck his head out the window, his hair flying straight back. His face pulled tight, and his eyes watered from the force of the wind.

Insomnia

"WE CAN'T just put him up on a horse and expect him to ride," I tell my husband, Clarence. "The man's almost a hundred years old. He ain't rode a horse in decades." I'm talking about Bob John Wheeler, owner of this dude ranch we just moved on. We pulled up with our trailer one day looking for work, and he says we can stay. Easy as that. But it's no picnic. He and his son, Jamie, stay in the main house, huge, all to themselves, and me and my family got to stay out here in this damn trailer parked next to the horse barn. We got a good deal on it, though. Lime green and silver Airliner for 350 dollars. We couldn't pass it up. Clarence'd been on unemployment for over a year, so we up and went. Barbie and Nancy whined the whole ride, said they wouldn't make any friends out here in the middle of the Ozarks. Kids think they know everything.

"Well, Mildred, you tell him then, I ain't telling him." Clarence waves his palms at me, no way. "Second thought, maybe we should get him up there riding, get him some fresh air. Maybe'll put him to sleep for once at night." Clarence and Bob John don't get on too well. Clarence says I spend way too much time worrying about him and waiting on him hand and foot. That's just because of Bob John's insomnia. The man can't sleep. Almost a hundred years old and he can't sleep. So I go in there in that musty, Vicksy room and talk to him about the weather and the horses and he starts telling me all about his wife, Glenda, may she rest in peace, and how the two of them used to win all the horse shows in Little Rock with their twin Arabians. "Been a slew of years've passed, but I still remember clear as a bell. I got pictures," he says, wheezing after every few words. I cover him up with blankets, smelling to cedar they been stored away so long.

So, last night I was up at the house, and he gets the idea he wants to go riding again. I ignored him, sung him a lullaby instead, but he got all agitated. Went on and on. How he wants Clarence to take him up through the trail again, up through what we named Bluefoot Paradise Trail. That's the trail we take visitors and tourists through with the horses. Twenty-five dollars a day, including a meal. Bob John's got maybe twenty horses in all, and they aren't good for much except slow trail riding. Most of them are Arabian grannies. Bony with big sagging bellies. But it's a living. I make the meals, Clarence tends the horses and leads trail rides. Barbie and Nancy are supposed to help with the horses, but they've taken to staying in town after school and going over to Vicki Secrest's place. Only thing is they miss the bus and Clarence or myself has to go traipsing into town, seven miles, and pick them up. But I got things to do. I said two trips a week now, that's it. I did pick me up a nice steam table when I went to fetch them last week. The girls were waiting for me at the Sparkle Cafe, and when I went inside, I saw Mr. Tracy hauling one out to the garbage. "You throwing that away?" I asked. He nodded. "Mind if I take it off your hands?" "Be my guest." He even carried it out to the car for me. So now I got something decent to keep meals hot for our riders. It's Monday, our slowest day usually, and we only had one group Clarence took up earlier today. I grab a rake that's leaning against our trailer and start creating a pile. Bob John likes it spic and span. Jamie sits out on the porch reading. All that big guy does is read. The man is almost sixty-five years old and I swear he never left this farm. I think something's not quite right in his head, but I don't say nothing. I hear Bob John hollering from inside the house.

"Son, get in here and help me. Got to get me some fresh air." His voice wavers out into the wind. His room is in the front of the house, and we keep the windows open so we can hear him if he needs anything. Jamie slams his book shut and sighs like a big heifer.

"It's getting chilly out, Pa," he says into the screen. "You just stay in there and rest." Jamie settles back in his chair, yawns, digs in his nose with his thumb, then after carefully examining the find, he wipes it on the pant of his overalls. I shake my head and walk over to the porch. Jamie doesn't notice me as I walk up the wooden stairs.

"I'll help your father if it's such a big stink," I say and slam the screen door behind me. Bob John is sitting up in his bed with a creamy blanket over his legs. He's not crippled, but his old bones just don't hold him up no more. He's a twig of a man, too. I help him slide into his wheelchair. It's not one of them metal electronic ones, but a deep-backed wooden chair with huge spoked wheels like an old tricycle. "It was my pop's," he told me when I first saw it. "Ain't it a beaut?" It is a beaut. I cover up his legs with the creamy blanket and wheel him through the kitchen and out onto the porch. Jamie hits his fist on his knee.

"I would've gotten ya, Pa, if you'da just given me a minute." He talks like a big child. "I's just in the middle of a sentence." Trouble is, ever since we got here, Jamie's been reading that same book, *How To Skin a Mink,* as if he's ever going to use that. Bob John cusses under his breath and laughs to himself, pounding his tiny fist on the arm of his chair. In some ways Jamie seems older than his father, his mind dull and rotten. Bob John's always on the go, at least mentally. And though they both got gray heads, I swear Jamie's is all the whiter and older looking.

I sit on the steps with my back to both of them and sigh. The sun's just about to set and it goes down fast here. Blink your eyes and you miss it. Over by the barn, I see Clarence's strong back lift saddles off the horses and throw them onto wooden beams. Then he pulls the plaid blankets off their backs and folds them in fours.

"So when you taking me riding?" Bob John asks, then hacks into his hanky.

"Well, I never did say I was taking you riding, now did I? I got lots to do, you know?" Jamie looks up at me, but when our eyes meet, he nosedives his face back into his book. "It's a pretty tough ride, Bob John."

"I know that! Who do you think blazed the damn trail?" Course he didn't, but that doesn't matter. He rubs his hands back and forth on his knees and grinds his teeth. "Tomorrow. We'll go riding tomorrow."

"But it's been years, you said so yourself. What makes you want to go riding again after all these years?" I try to reason him out of it. Then he'll forget where he's coming from altogether.

He leans down toward me and whispers, "A man's got to get some fresh air. He's got to get out and enjoy the fresh air. To everything there is a season, a time, a place . . ." He starts rattling Ecclesiastes at me, until he drops off to a nap. I glare at Jamie, still reading in the half-dark.

"Some help you are," I say. "You know he can't go riding anymore at his age. Why didn't you say something?"

He shrugs his shoulders. "Dunno. His ranch. He can do whatever he wants." He bobs his head down to the book. I'm about to hit the ape of a son when I see our girls being dropped off at the gate in a blue truck. "Bye!" they yell with light voices, and the truck tears off, blowing dust behind it. I stand up, flagging them over. Bob John shakes in his sleep. He sleeps through anything, except at night. "Who's that brought you home?" The girls swing their books and laugh. "Vicki's brother, Paul. He goes hunting around here," Nancy tells me and they both laugh again. "What's so funny in that?" I say, smiling, crossing my arms. "Nothing," they both say and elbow each other. I'm not stupid. One of them likes him. Probably Nancy, but she's only twelve years old. I'll have to talk to them soon about boys who are old enough to drive.

"Well, let's go get us some supper," I say, and put an arm around each girl. I give Jamie a final glare that goes unnoticed. Bum son, I think. "Clarence!" I holler across the field. "Supper in about ten minutes." He lifts up his hand that he's heard.

The girls get plates and tumblers. I taught them young to help their ma. I never got away with nothing when I was young. Made supper for the family every night. Even if I had a boy to see after supper, I had to stay and wash dishes.

My kitchen is cramped and small, so I try fixing easy things that don't take lots of time. Tonight we're having noodles in cream of mushroom soup with cut-up beans and carrots. Sara Lee pound cake for dessert. Clarence is a big eater, course you'd never know by looking at him. Narrow boyish hips, long friendly face, gangly arms and legs. That's how it is with men. Me, I got to watch every blessed thing I eat.

"Barbie, go call your father. Tell him dinner's on." She leans out the screen door and hollers.

"Now, I coulda done that," I say, putting the carton of milk on the table. All it takes for Clarence to fly is food, and in no time at all, he's in the kitchen, head almost poking through the ceiling. He takes off his hat, his gloves, kicks off the boots full of feed. He sits down at the table and rubs his hands.

"Clarence, aren't you forgetting your manners?" He never washes his hands, which bothers me. All that grimy horse hair and dung all over and he don't think to wash up. "Clarence! Shoo!" I wave him over to the sink and he washes reluctantly. Finally, we say grace.

"So, honey, did you tell the old man we ain't taking him riding?" Clarence has already gulped down two glasses of milk and his plate is half empty.

"Well, sure I told him, but he doesn't listen. You know Bob John. He fell into a nap as we was talking about it. Dumb son just sat there like a rock. Said, 'Aw, it's his farm, can do what he wants.' I don't know what he thinks he's doing out here, sitting on his rearend all day." The girls are picking tiny pieces of mushroom out of their hotdish, and also the carrots and beans.

"Well, you better tell him he's not going, 'cause I ain't taking him." Clarence sits back in his chair and rubs his belly.

"Well, Bob John said 'Tomorrow, we're going tomorrow.' That's what he said, Clarence. But I'm giving him a haircut tonight, I'll try to talk him out of it." I shrug my shoulders at him, and start eating my hotdish, which has gotten cold and gummy.

After supper Clarence flicks on the black-and-white tv on the kitchen counter. He unrolls his tobacco and thumbs some down into his pipe — mahogany wood carved into a squarish horsehead. It was a gift from his father, who was a prize-winning horseman himself. Clarence loves it; it's his after-dinner ritual. The girls lie on the tiny living room floor, paging through the Sears catalogue. "I'm going to cut Bob John's hair, Clarence. Why don't you come by later? Visit with him a little?" He sucks the last from his pipe and blows smoke rings up into the light. "Mildred, come 'ere." He motions me over with two fingers. He pulls me down on his lap and kisses my lips right on. "Mildred, honey, I love you, but I don't think we need to make such a fuss about that old man. Just give him his haircut, and make sure and tell him he's not going riding tomorrow." I roll my eyes and wonder just who Clarence thinks he is. Telling me what to do.

"See you later," I say and leave them there with the dirty dishes. I'll take any chance I can to get out of that damn trailer. It's no house. It's a little box with roll-open windows. I hate it.

I knock and Jamie yells come in with a booming voice. Bob John sits in his wheelchair next to Jamie on the couch watching "Charlie's Angels". Bob John is laughing toothless. They don't even look to see I've come in.

"Looka them girls shoot," Bob John pipes to Jamie, whose face remains glazed and absorbed.

"Ready for that haircut, Bob John?" He turns around but doesn't see me, then turns back to the tv. "I said, you ready for that haircut, Bob John?"

"Pa, Mildred's here for your haircut. Just take him, Mildred." I raise my eyebrows at the uppity-doody directions, and wheel Bob John toward the kitchen. The linoleum'll be easier to clean up than that nubby scarlet shag in the living room.

"Hey, hey, hey!" Bob John yells as he's wheeled away from the tv screen. "I'm watchin' something!" So I roll him into the kitchen but turn him around to face the tv in the living room. This seems to satisfy him. I go to the bathroom and grab a black comb and sharp silver scissors. In the kitchen, I fill up a tall glass of water.

"Keep still now," I say, holding his head straight. I dip the comb in the water and slide it through his hair. Soft gray strands stick to his neck. I press them down with my fingers and snip off about an inch.

"Don't let that itchy hair in my collar," he fidgets and brushes at his neck.

"Bob John, keep still I said." I grab a dishtowel out of the drawer, wrap it tight around his neck, and stick the extra down his shirt.

"And short, I like it short," he says and crosses his arms.

"I know," I sigh loudly and Jamie looks over to check up on us. Bob John's got less than a monk's ring of stringy hair and it only takes a few minutes to trim. The cup of water floats tiny dashes of gray at the top. I stand with my hand on my hips and examine.

"Done already? Ya can't be done already. A good cut takes time." He feels around his head with red wrinkled fingers. "All right, all right, but what about the horse ride tomorrow? You talk to that husband of yours? I want to do that trail ride tomorrow."

"It looks good, your hair looks real pretty," I say, "if I do say so myself." He scowls at me, then coughs until I think he's choking to death. Jamie starts moving from the couch.

"I'm all right, all right," Bob John says, and waves his hands. "Don't worry about me none. I'm all right. Going riding tomorrow."

"Well, you better get some sleep then," I say, and start wheeling him toward the bedroom before he can protest. His room is dark and smells like lotion and peppermint candies. I help him out of his chair and onto the bed, where

he curls like an old snail. I peel off his blue velvet slippers
and pull the covers over him. The back of his head is still
damp as I reach to adjust the pillow.

"Good night," I say.

"Yeah, yeah, g'night then," he mumbles.

When I come into the kitchen, Jamie is sitting at the table
with a wet head and a big terry towel bunched around his
neck. Water drips down his face and onto his pants.

"Thought maybe I could get my hairs cut, Mrs.
Wooters." Well, what can I say to that? So I go back into the
bathroom and get the scissors. Thing is, I don't like Jamie
so much. He don't help his poor father any and he don't do
nothing himself either except read about mink. "I already
got a cup of water," he says as I come back with the scissors.
"And a comb." The idea of cutting Jamie's hair kinda gets
me. It's not smooth and soft and gray like Bob John's, but
coarse and matted and no tellin' what's in it. His hair
doesn't even absorb water; drops just go dribbling right off
like it's metal or something.

"Now sit still," I say, holding his chin, "How short you
want it?" It's pretty long for an old man. He holds up his
thumb and finger and shows me about an inch. So I start
cutting off some slack first, and they fall in puffs like tiny
sos pads.

"You're pretty," Jamie says as I'm combing down his
bangs. I don't respond, so he says it again, "You're pretty."

"Well, now, I'm nothing but ordinary looking, but thank
you, Jamie." He smiles gold-capped teeth, and this makes
me nervous.

"You're nice even if you don't let my dad go riding," he
says and touches my hand. I quickly pull it away and stand
back to inspect what I've done so far.

"Well, looks like we're almost done here," I say. "It's
getting late already. I gotta be gettin' home to see if my girls

are in bed yet 'cause they got school tomorrow, you know."
I bend my knees and pull up close to his ears with the
scissors to cut the fine hair by his sideburns.

"I like you," he says, and before I know what's happening, he tries planting a big kiss on my cheek. Reacting in a
panic, the hand holding the scissors jerks and I cut him
right across the cheek. I don't mean to do it, really. But
there's blood on his cheek, just a thin line, and he looks at
me confused. Then he touches his cheek, looks at his hand,
and starts hollering at the top of his lungs.

"Jamie, now hush up, it's only a tiny cut. Now what'd
you think you were doing anyways?" I grab a Kleenex in
the bathroom and give it to him to dab on the cut. Then I
hear Bob John start up in the bedroom. Mumbling how he
wants to get up, what's going on, somebody get him out of
his damn bed. But I'm not bothering with him. Got enough
on my hands here with Jamie bawling and hollering.

"My dad wants to get up," Jamie says, and looks at me
sideways. "You better help him." He holds the big terry
towel up to his face in a ball. You'd think I slit his throat or
something the way he's carrying on.

"Listen, here, Jamie, I didn't even hurt you hardly," I
say, standing in front of the refrigerator. "You're the one
who's looking for trouble." Bob John is still rustling around
the bedroom and spouting out demands I don't intend to
follow. I toss out the water from the haircuts and start
sweeping up before I go home. Jamie is pouting like a two-
year-old.

"Lemme see it if it's so bad," I say, reaching for Jamie's
towel on his face.

"No, leave me alone!"

"Just let me see if it's all right before I go home."

"No." He goes over to the couch and lays down. I stand
above him.

"Jamie, you listen to me. Just let me see — " Then we hear a loud crash and then a thud from Bob John's bedroom. Jamie sits up. Neither of us says anything.

"That better not be your pa, Jamie, 'cause if it is this is all your fault." I start slowly toward the bedroom.

"It is not," Jamie says. "It's yours." He starts coming toward the bedroom, but I point my finger at him and tell him to stay out.

In Bob John's bedroom it's dark, but I can see him, his small body curled the same as it was in bed, only he's on the floor twisted in the afghan. He looks pale all over, glowing. And the moon that shines in makes him glow even more. I touch the hair on the back of his head, but jump back as Bob John starts flailing his hands this way and that.

"Hey, what about helpin' me up here instead of breathin' down my neck." He peels the afghan off and tries reaching up to the bed. Man scared me half to death. Now he's hollering at me to help him, help him. Well, I'll help him, but I know what's coming next. When we going riding, when we going riding? I have a mind to just take the old cat riding and be done with it. Lord, he's stubborn.

I help him up into his wheelchair and bring him out to the living room where Jamie is still watching tv. He has plastered a Band-Aid across his cheek and holds his thick hand over it to make it seem worse.

"Aw, Jamie, what's happened to you now?" Bob John shouts across the living room, and before they get bickering, I decide to get the hell outta there.

"Well, you take care now, Bob John. Hope ya'll get some sleep tonight." I nod good-bye to Jamie real cold-like and head toward the trailer. Nancy and Barbie ought to have done them dishes by now, and God help them, if they didn't, Clarence'd better well done them. It sounds awful quiet as I walk up the steps, and inside the trailer all them dirty dishes are still sitting there and the tv's on and no-body's watching it and Clarence is nowhere to be seen, just Nancy, yakking on the phone.

"Where's your father?" I ask, and put away the milk that's been left on the table to sour. She wrinkles her eye-brows and shoos me away with her hand. "Listen to me now, miss," but she hovers over the phone deeper. So I stand right next to her and wait with my arms crossed until she gets real nervous and finally says she has to go and hangs up.

"Now what's going on here? Where's Barbie and your pa? And why aren't these damn dishes done? You'd think somebody could lend me a hand around here once. The milk's going sour it's been sitting so long." A big pause. "Huh?"

"Well, I was gonna do them but we were just doing something and I forgot." Nancy looks at all the dishes on the table and shakes her head. Something's up, now I know these things the minute I look into her eyes. Something's definitely up.

"What's the matter here? Sit down, tell me what's the matter." I pat the back of a kitchen chair. "Where's your pa?"

Nancy sits on the edge of the chair. She scrapes at a dirty plate with a fork. "Umm, he's gone. He's out looking for Barbie."

"For Barb? Now where in heaven's Barb gone off to? I thought the two of you had schoolwork to do. Where'd she go?" I start cleaning up the table; that's how it is when I'm upset. I can't just sit there and look at all the mess. Now I had a feeling something wasn't quite right all day long. I stack the crusted plates and squirt a little Ivory in the sink full of hot water.

"Well, we don't know where Barb went, Mom." Nancy starts helping me, scraping the leftovers from the casserole into an old Parkay container. I whirl around. "What? What are you talking about now, Nancy? Don't fool with me." I stare her in the eye as I wipe dry the dishes. "Well, don't get mad at her, but I think Paul called and she went out somewhere with him." Nancy says this quietly, as if Barbie is around.

"Paul? Who's Paul? Oh, now wait a minute, is he the boy brought you two home today? The boy that can drive?"

"Yeah."

"How old is he anyways?"

"I don't know. Maybe sixteen or seventeen."

"Lord Jesus, who does she think she is! I never said she could be going out on any school night and I ain't never said she could be going out with any sixteen-year-old boy!" I walk into the living room to check the clock. "It's nearly 11:30. What're they up to anyway? I sure wish Clarence were here."

So me and Nancy wash and dry the dishes in silence and wipe off the counters and sit at the kitchen table with our hands flat on the damp tablecloth. All's we can do is wait. It's strange, not realizing how old the girls are getting. They just seem so little together, laying around the house, walking off to the school bus, but I guess they're growing up. Though I can't imagine Barbie with no older boy. She's so shy she don't even know what to say to her father sometimes. Then again, maybe this wasn't even her idea. Thinking this gets me so nervous I keep checking the windows to see if Clarence is on his way home.

About 1:00 a.m. Nancy finally drifts off to sleep on the living room floor watching tv. Just as I'm about to go into the bedroom and start undressing for bed, I hear the pickup spitting up the gravel driveway. I run out the door and cross my arms in the cold to wait for him to come in. There's another little figure in the truck, so I sigh relief, least he's got Barbie. But Clarence gets out, and Barbie stays in the cab. Clarence waves me over to the truck. It's the middle of fall so it's pretty cold, but I go over in my bare feet with no jacket. Clarence puts his arm around me.

"Barbie's scared you gonna yell at her so she's stayin' in the truck." Well, if I ever heard of anything more stupid, I don't know.

"That's ridiculous, Clarence. What's the matter? Where was she, for god's sake?" I walk over to the passenger door and motion Barbie to come out. But Clarence takes me aside.

"See, she's had a little bit to drink," Clarence says, "and she's a little sick."

"Drinkin'? She's only twelve years old! Clarence, for god's sake, what's going on here?" I walk over to the truck and open the door and tell Barbie to get out now and come into the house. No sense in us all freezing out here.

So we do. Barbie lurks behind us and we wait at the kitchen table for her. I keep looking at Clarence like he's gonna tell me something so I know what's going on here, but he avoids my eyes and keeps looking at his watch. Then Barbie comes in, looking a little bleary-eyed and Clarence tells her to go to sleep, we'll talk about it in the morning.

"Clarence! What do you think you're doing? Nancy told me she was out with that Paul Secrest, you know, who drives them home sometimes. Now where'd she get the idea she could go out gallivanting like that, huh?" I pound on the table with two fingers, but Clarence gets up and mumbles something. "What was that, Clarence?"

"I said, did you get the old bastard to sleep tonight?" He turns around and smiles at me funny, like he's made a big joke.

"Well, yes, I'm sure he's just sleeping fine by now. What's that got to do with anything?" Clarence tries to kick off his boots but he can't. "Clarence, have you been drinking? You haven't been drinking, have you?"

He turns around and laughs. His whole body teeters and he laughs again at himself. "Mildred, it don't matter, does it? It just don't matter to you." He goes off toward the bedroom, but I'm following him.

"Clarence, you tell me what's going on with Barbie. She could've gotten herself in trouble or something."

"Yeah, but she didn't. I told her she could go. So what do you care? You ain't here to see to anything, always up at the damn house . . ."

"What are you talking about? Clarence, don't try pulling my leg with that jealous routine about Bob John, 'cause if you're jealous of a hundred-year-old man, you got some heck of a problem." Clarence is stripping down to his boxer shorts and lays down on the bed to pull off his pants. "Barbie can't have no dates until she's older. You hear me, Clarence, you—"

"I hear you, Mildred, but I'd like to get some sleep, please." And with that he falls off to sleep and leaves me sitting there, real mad. And Barbie drunk in her bedroom. That Clarence—this ain't happened in a long time, his drinking. But I gotta leave this house. I can't stay in this trailer no more. And tomorrow I'm gonna do it, too. Swear to god I'm gonna, and maybe I'll just take Bob John for that trail ride before I do.

What We Found

I watch the cook slice tomatoes and lay them over salad greens. He hands me the plates and asks what I'm doing later. I don't answer. He knows better. I see my table of gray-haireds are restless with empty glasses. They are one of four tables in the restaurant and we are almost ready to close. Matt walks in, looking frantic. Matt's my younger brother.

"Hannah," he whispers, "you have to get out of here." I stop and try to gauge his panic. Matt tends to hyper-react to most situations. His hair is blown over to one side of his head. "It's Will."

"Will?"

"Yeah, I found Will."

"What? What are you talking about? I have to wait on these tables." Matt sits in an empty booth and waits for me. I wait for people to finish eating. I keep looking at Matt, but he won't look at me.

After twenty minutes of pouring coffee, clearing plates and rolling silverware, I'm worried and decide there is no more time to wait, so I leave with Matt and ask Sara to close up. Matt drives our parents' old car – a blue Nova with no muffler. I hate driving in the blue Nova because of the noise. Matt goes fast. I keep my hands on the dash.

"Matt, what happened?" I want to know about Will. I love Will. We have been living together for the past seven years.

"Just wait until we get there." Matt's nervous; he's hiding something, I can tell. Matt's my best friend.

Last Saturday he picked me up from work about 1:30 a.m. Matt's a janitor at McCall State Bank, so he works his own hours at night. I had to stay late at the restaurant to clean and set up for the next day. I've been a waitress for nearly ten years. Then we went to the river and Matt pulled two King Kans of beer out of a paper bag. We downed them and sat there until the sun came up. We talked about our mother, who died exactly three months ago. Matt started crying. I helped him through.

Now we are out on a tiny gravel road right outside of McCall, near the river. There are tire tracks everywhere and wet matted grass. Matt stops the car and rests his forehead on the steering wheel. He accidentally hits the horn and we both jump.

"Matt, what is it?" He won't tell me anything, so I get out of the car. The dew on the tall weeds chills my bare legs. I'm still in my waitress uniform – a too-short brown skirt and faded matching blouse.

"Hannah, follow me." Matt strides quickly through the dark with me stumbling after. He keeps stopping, saying, "I'm here, I'm over here," to make sure I keep up.

Matt lives in Mom's old house now. We don't have a father, not one that we know of anyway. Since we are the only children, the house was willed to us after she died. I had already moved in with Will; Matt wanted to stay in the house. He didn't want to sell it, as I'd suggested. I still go visit. Usually Sundays I go over in the late afternoon and make Matt and me some supper, maybe spaghetti or barbecued chicken. We read the paper and talk and watch "60 Minutes." Matt settles down then, is more at peace than usual.

Matt stops suddenly and touches my shoulder. I feel something bad and hold my stomach. Matt tells me to take a look. There is Will lying in the grass. I put my hand over my mouth and look up at the sky. So many stars; a clear night. Matt turns to me. He knows what's happened, what's happening.

I am twenty-nine. Ten years ago I was going out with Tommy Dyrud and I got pregnant. I had the baby a month early, and she died two weeks later. I named her Laurel Kay and she was lovely. Tommy left for college in California shortly after that, with apologies and kisses. I was glad he left. I never cried throughout the whole ordeal; I thought I felt relieved. Then one day while waiting for my appointment at the clinic, a man introduced himself, Will, and told me he couldn't help noticing that I had the prettiest eyes he had ever seen. And what color were they? I told him they were green, and he said, Ah, spruce. He asked me if I would have lunch with him. We went. I didn't think anything of it at the time. He was much older than me and I certainly wasn't looking for anyone. But I swear I fell in love that day. We spent the rest of the afternoon kissing on his couch. He asked me to stay over, but that was when my mother was getting sick and I had to go. Will understood. He called me twice that night to see if I was all right. He thought I looked too pale. I said, No, I felt fine.

While my mother was practically decaying, I was filling up with this incredible lightness. Will and I spent the next day at the public library, reading about my mother's illness, cancer of the thorax. I asked Will what he did for a living and he took me out to lunch again to tell me.

He was a priest once, but quit when he was thirty-two years old because he didn't believe in it anymore. My mouth kept opening and closing, saying, No way, no way. I felt like I was cheating somehow, sinning. Now he teaches English at the parochial high school I graduated from eleven years ago. I told him I felt guilty, that maybe I should leave him alone. He took my hand and said, "No, please don't do that." Then I went home to my mother who couldn't even speak anymore.

Two months later, Will asked me to move in with him. He lived in a one-story brick house in town. I didn't hesitate. My mother couldn't talk to me or focus. Maybe I was getting scared and just wanted someone to take care of me, but I loaded all my things in Will's pickup and moved in. My first night there I found two big down pillows on the bed, on my side, because I couldn't sleep on the flat foam ones Will preferred. I laid my head onto them and felt such complete comfort and relief. I slept on my side. Will learned to sleep with his hand in the small of my back.

Three months later it was summer and I quit my job. I wasn't making any tips and felt exhausted. That day Matt started acting up. He had just finished high school, had absolutely no plans and wanted to kill himself. He wrote me good-bye notes and taped them to our door. In them, he said I was his only friend and he felt like he was losing me and also losing himself. He said the man who gets to marry me is the luckiest man. He refused to see a psychologist—not that we could afford it, with Mom in and out of the hospital continuously.

One day the hospital called me and told me they were going to have to remove her larynx and thorax in parts and they needed my permission since she wasn't coherent anymore. I walked up to the hospital, stopping every once in a while to lean on mailboxes. It was a hundred degrees that day. When the doctor gave me the papers, I shook my head. They said it had to be done to keep her with us. It was spreading and they needed to arrest it. After two hours of watching her struggle to breathe, I signed the papers, my hand heavy as cement. I ran into the bathroom and laid my cheek on the cool tile wall, then threw up. When I came home, Will was making tomato soup and grilled cheese sandwiches. He was in a good mood, laughing, but when I saw the Adam's apple in his throat move up and down as he talked, I ran to the bathroom. When I told Will about it later, he put his hand to my forehead and checked for a fever. He said he understood. He always understood. He held my hand and we watched tv until we both fell asleep on the couch.

"Hannah, we have to move him." Matt pulls my sleeve. It is dark and the weeds rustle with a cold autumn wind. I feel like I'm falling.

"Where? Where will we move him?"

"To our place. I don't know. But we have to move him."

We hoist Will's body over us and against us and awkwardly carry him to the car. Matt carries most of the weight. He was a wrestler in high school—big, hard body, barrel-chested. I wonder if Will is dead, but the thought turns cruel and comical in my head and I start dropping him.

"Hold on, Hannah." Matt opens the back door with one hand. Burrs and thistles scrape my legs. The hem of my skirt is wet.

"I can't."

Somehow we get him into the backseat. We start driving through fog patches with the high beams on. I can't decide if this is true or joke or dream, but Matt moves, shifts gears, breathes heavily, so it's true.

"Where are we going?" I wail. Panicked for a minute, I forget everything.

"We'll go to our place. To Mom's."

"Is he dying?" Silence. "Matt!"

"What?" he parks the Nova. There are no lights on in the house. I remember Mom taping notes all over – TURN OFF THE LIGHTS, DON'T LEAVE WATER RUNNING, CLOSE THE RE- FRIGERATOR DOOR.

"Doesn't it feel weird living here, Matt? So alone."

"You're probably in shock, so you don't know what you're talking about. Come on in the house."

We carry Will into the house. I have never carried anything so heavy. He's like a huge bag of sand. We struggle through the door, stop once for a breath in the door- way, then lay him on the couch. He is wearing a flannel shirt, a jean jacket, a blue scarf. He is breathing. He's forty- one years old. His face is deep red and white in spots. I touch it.

Matt wipes sweat off his own forehead. He sits on his knees like a small child. He does not look at Will, he looks at me, then closes his eyes.

"I'll tell you about it later," he sighs. "Will'll be okay."

Matt has always been uncomfortable around Will. When- ever Matt would come over, he'd sit in the kitchen, Will in the living room with me. Only I'd keep walking back and forth, trying to bridge things. Matt didn't have a job then, which made things worse. He lived at Mom's, whenever she was home from the hospital, and read to her all day

long. Agatha Christie mysteries, Robert Frost, *Time* magazine, the local paper. I always worried about him. He'd call
me up at strange hours, usually very early in the morning,
around 5:00. "Hannah," he'd whisper, "please understand." "Understand what?" I'd ask, Will sound asleep beside me. "Understand how hard all of this is for me." Then
Matt would start crying and I'd tell him to come over. Soon
I'd hear the Nova in the driveway. Will was a heavy sleeper
and never woke up. I'd crawl out of the warm bed to let
Matt in and make him a place on the couch. Soft blankets,
an afghan, pillows from the extra bed. The sun would be
just blinking through the blinds and light the room a dim
orange. The refrigerator hummed. I'd sit on the floor until
Matt fell asleep. The room brightened. By that time Will
would be moving around the bedroom, and I'd hear the
shower spritz on and Will's deep singing.

Will wasn't angry about Matt, but I knew he was
concerned. He asked about Matt's past, our childhood. If
anything happened to him as a kid. I told him no, nothing
happened, except we never had a father and Matt always
wished we had a father, but that was all, nothing
happened.

Matt throws a blanket over Will. He walks into the kitchen
and opens the refrigerator. He clanks pans and dishes.
"Matt, what are you doing in there? Come here." I call to
him. I touch Will's arm and feel for a pulse. It's there, steady
and slow. He is warm and actually looks comfortable in
peaceful sleep. I start crying. "What are you doing, Matt?
Come in here and talk to me!"

"You come in here," Matt says. In the kitchen he is making pancakes. Dirty dishes are scattered everywhere. In the
sink, pans full of dingy water float old food.

"Why are you making pancakes now?" I want to kill him. I want to know what's wrong with Will. Maybe he had a heart attack. I run back to him in the living room. Matt turns on the radio to news. "Turn that off, Matt, and quit making pancakes."

"Hannah, I wish you'd believe me. Everything's going to be all right."

"How do you know? You don't know. How did you find him? I mean, how would you know to look down by the river? Did he tell you he was going there? I don't know why he'd be down there so late. Matt, get in here!" I start crying hysterically.

"Hannah, don't cry." Matt comes into the living room and wipes his hands on his pants. He has a wet dishtowel hung from his belt loop. He takes my hand and leads me to the kitchen table. "Hannah, why don't you let me make you something to eat? Then we can talk. It's nothing to worry about. I'd tell you if it was, you know?" I nod. "So don't worry, okay?"

"Matt," I say, "quit it." He brings me a wad of toilet paper to wipe my nose. For a moment I relax and forget about Will on the couch. I think back to my mother's death, her hands bunching the sheets, her last sloping sighs. I watch Matt's big hands crack eggs. His thick fingers slow and awkward with the shell. He turns to me and smiles. For a second it feels right to be back home with Matt, making breakfast, except that our mother is missing and it's 3:30 in the morning, and Will.

When I was ten and Matt was eight we decided to run away. Matt said he would be the dad and I would be the mom, and we would be like pioneers. We packed a big garbage bag full of blankets and saltines and candles and our walkie-talkies from the Christmas before. It was winter and below freezing, but Matt said we had to go. I just wanted to make Matt happy, but I was nervous and afraid our mom would get mad.

We said we were going out to feed the dog and check on him, but walked straight down to Jenkin's Creek to the green shed Matt had found for us. He always hung around by that creek and built forts. The green shack was deserted except for some rusty tools and wood scraps. It had a cold dirt floor. Matt climbed through the open window and helped me in. I was afraid someone would catch us and tell. I was always afraid. Matt laid the blankets out on the dirt floor and said, "Here, let's lay down and warm up." We did. We wore layers of clothes and scarves and mittens, but it was still freezing. We laid together like spoons; me in front, Matt huddled up against my back. He lit a candle, but only for a minute, in case anyone saw.

"Don't put it out," I pleaded.

"We have to," Matt ordered.

I started to feel numb all over. I persisted, "Matt, let's go. This isn't fun anymore."

"I know it isn't fun," he said, "but we have to do it."

"Why do we have to do it?" I asked. He told me we couldn't be happy in our house, but I didn't understand.

We both dozed off for a while, then, waking up fuzzy later, I heard car tires crunching through the snow and saw lights through the wooden boards of the shed. "Matt," I whispered, "maybe it's Mom looking for us."

"Maybe," he whispered. But he didn't want to leave. He told me he never wanted to leave. "Pretty soon we'll wake up and it will be sunny and warm and we can go somewhere else." He paused. "I love you, Hannah. Please stay."

I stayed for a while, but then I couldn't move my hands or toes and started crying. "Matt, I can't feel anything at all," I cried. "I'm frozen!"

"Here, give me your hands. I'll warm them up," Matt suggested. But it didn't work and we ended up walking home in the dark with stiff limbs and runny noses. I don't know how long we had been gone. Maybe it was a few hours, but our mother was hysterical. She had been out looking for us and had the police on the phone when we walked in the door.

I was crying so hard that Mom thought something had happened to us. "No, Mom, no one hurt us," I said. "I'm just cold." Matt went right to his room, but Mom made me sit down and tell her what happened, because I was the oldest. I didn't know what to say. I sat there and shivered in my t-shirt and underpants under layers of fuzzy blankets while Mom questioned me. "It was all Matt's idea," I confessed, and looked at his bedroom door. "We're sorry."

We are through eating pancakes. I have eaten two bites. Matt eats more heartily.

"How can you just sit there and eat?" I ask him.

"Easy," he answers. "I'm hungry."

"Now tell me the story, Matt. You have to. You said you would."

"Just a sec," he says, but the phone rings. Matt looks at me, then at the phone. "I'll get it," he says, and answers it in the dining room. "Hello? Yeah, this is. Mmm-hmm. Oh, hi. How are you? Mmm-hmm. No, actually I haven't. No. No. Oh, really, I don't know. That could be. Oh, she's fine. Yeah, she's been busy."

I stand right next to Matt and point my finger at myself and mouth "Me?" Matt waves me away, then I realize it must be for Will. I go into Mom's bedroom and pick up the other phone.

"Hello? Who's this?" It's Will's brother, Terry, from Ontario. "Hi, Terry." He asks me if I've seen Will because he's been trying to get ahold of him all night. Before I can answer, Matt cuts us off. He clicks the phone up and down until there is a loud beeping. I run out to the dining room. "Matt, what did you do that for? God, he was looking for Will. What are you trying to prove?"

"Let's go for a drive, Hannah. Come on, then we can talk." He waits for a response. "Really. I love you. I don't want to upset you."

"Why did you hang up on Terry?" I ask. Then I see that he has left the phone off the hook. I slam it back down. I go toward Will on the couch, then stop. "I'm not leaving," I tell Matt as he slips into his coat.

"Well, I am," he answers and waits by the front door.

"Where are you going?" I ask stupidly. "No, go ahead and go. I'm going to call a doctor." I stand to face him. "I'm not going to let you do this to me. Don't do this, Matt. Just go. Get out of here."

Matt leans against the door. "Hannah, I was with Will tonight."

"You were?" I ask.

He nods. "That's all I'm going to say until we leave this house."

"We are not leaving this house!" I scream. Then I start crying again. I feel so helpless. Matt smiles. "It's not funny!" I yell at him.

"Just settle down," he says. "It'll be okay." We sit down at the dining room table and I put my head down on my arms. I can't see why any of this is happening.

After they removed Mom's thorax and larynx parts, she became worse. It became harder and harder to go visit her.

Her eyes reflected the pain she felt inside. She didn't speak, just squinted her watery blue eyes. She never cried, except the time I came in with violets and told her I needed her more than anything else in the world, and that she simply could not die. She closed her eyes and tears came through. I held her hand and ran my other hand up and down the soft inside of her arm. Her skin had loosened and felt papery and cool to the touch. "Mom," I told her, "you are a strong woman with plenty of years left. Hold on." She couldn't answer me, but she took her fingertips and gently ran them over my eyelids and nose and lips until I wanted to go to sleep.

The day after the operation, she didn't wake up for several hours. I thought she was dead, even though the doctor had told me she might need two to three days to regain consciousness. I walked slowly through the hospital and looked at the babies and listened to all the noise. I called Matt from a pay phone and told him to meet me in the cafeteria. I told him Mom had died. He was there in practically five minutes.

We sat on the orange plastic chairs and stared at two pieces of blueberry pie that neither of us touched.

"When did she die?" Matt asked. He smelled like sleep.

"Just now," I told him. He stared into my face without even seeing me. "I *think* she's dead, Matt. She hasn't woken up yet. I don't know."

"What?" He stood up and glared at me. "Hannah, don't ever do that. I'm going up to see Mom now." He started to walk away, but I followed.

In the room, Mom lay there with her eyelids flickering. Matt held me and cried. "God, Hannah, we're so lucky." Then he kissed Mom's cheek. We stood and watched them change gauze pads from her neck. Large pins held the fragile skin in place. Her mouth was covered with a breathing mask. A green dot jumped slowly on the black screen.

"You two going to be all right?" the doctor asked us. Neither one of us answered him. "All right then, good," he said, and left us alone.

Matt and I left for a while to get some fresh air, and felt relieved and hopeful. We drove the blue Nova out toward the river and opened the windows for some cool air. "You think she'll be okay?" Matt asked.

"I think so," I answered. But I remembered the way her head was tilted back, jerked off from the rest of her body. I wanted to hear her voice. I wanted her to sing Karen Carpenter's songs along with her records. I wanted her to say, "Now, Hannah," when she thought I was being unreasonable. But it was just Matt and me, and I was scared. I really thought she was dead after the operation. I leaned on Matt's shoulder and we drove and drove. He let me out at Will's house that night and I watched him drive away, fast.

Matt convinces me to go sit outside on the front steps, even though it is far too cold for that. I don't object; I don't care. Matt leads me out by the shoulders and I let him. I'm wearing an old coat of Mom's—a long camel hair. Matt knows I won't take his stalling much longer. I'm worried about Will but I don't know what to do. I'm also worried about Matt. But my panic has numbed me and paralyzed my thinking. Matt has a quick pulse behind all his actions, a suddenness that makes me anxious and scared. It's windy and brisk. I hear our garbage can blow over and roll across the backyard. Matt sticks his hands in his pockets and looks up.

"Hannah, look. It's starting to snow." I can only see it underneath the streetlight. Small silvery flakes. "It's barely October and it's already snowing. Can you believe that?" I don't answer. Matt rubs my back. "You okay?" I put my head down. My knees shake from the cold. "I'll go get you a hat and mittens, Hannah, okay?" He slams the door behind him. My knuckles bend stiff and white.

Matt comes back with a red beret and Mom's worn leather gloves. "This is all I could find," he apologizes, and lays them on my lap. I pull the beret down over my ears. I sit on my gloved hands and wait. The sky shifts to navy blue. Matt pulls out a bottle of Southern Comfort, drinks, then passes it to me. I turn my head the other way. He drinks again.

"This is good stuff," he says, "keeps you warm." He smiles. "Hannah," he says, "come on." I feel slow and weak, as if I'm being pulled. Matt rubs my knee, pats it like a grandparent would. "I tell you, Hannah, this is going to be okay. Everything's going to turn out okay. We're going to be okay." Then he grows serious and turns to face me.

"Okay, Matt," I say slowly. "Tell me exactly what happened to Will. Then we're taking him to the hospital."

"Well," he begins, "Will and I had a fight. Things have been pretty tense, you know? Maybe you don't know. Anyway, we had it out."

"Had it out?" I ask. "You mean you fought him?" He nods. "But why? You're way bigger than him, and stronger."

When I first met Will, I thought he was too stuffy and secure. But I had been losing ground, worn out from my mother's illness, and I welcomed his constancy. Everything in his house was solid and warm, and when I walked around all the dark woodwork, I felt whole, centered. I didn't mind doing dishes and sewing curtains for the windows, because to me it meant freedom and grace and becoming a part of something and someone else. My mother couldn't reach out to me anymore, she had no words, so I started spending all my time with Will. He was calm and loved me so much. I could see it in his eyes. Especially at night when we went to bed. He would watch as I smeared toothpaste on my brush, scrubbed up and down. He said I made him happy. He worried that he was too old for me. We talked about children. "It's not that I don't want to have any," he said. "It's just that I'm getting too old to be a father." I didn't care at the time; I was drained in that way. I had just lost a child and my mother was dying. Will was a good, steady man to go to bed with at night. I got to feel comfortable and safe lying next to him, warm flannel, his back never to me.

We went to bed early at first. This was safety for me, regularity I could count on. But it became harder and harder for me to sleep. When we turned out all the lights and the only sound was the refrigerator running, I'd turn to Will, pull up close to him and say, "Are you sleeping yet? Don't go to sleep until I do. Please. I can't stand being the only one awake." I knew it was a dumb thing to do, but I couldn't help it.

He was so good. He'd feel for my hand and say, "Don't worry, I'm here. Do you want to talk?" But pretty soon I'd fall asleep. It was unfair, me using Will to hold together.

He never came up to the hospital with me, though. He sent my mother cards and flowers, but he wouldn't come up to visit, not even on holidays, which bothered me. Our first Christmas together, we baked all kinds of cookies. I brought over recipes I found at Mom's house, and Will went to the store for flour and sugar and eggs and food coloring and colored sprinkles. We made Russian tea cakes, spritz, cut outs, fudge, turtles. I did most of the baking while Will took pictures of the whole ordeal, the whole mess. I remember him snapping away, flour prints all over his camera and pants. But I felt like a child, his child, so I started cleaning up. Will sensed it. I think he felt guilty for destroying the fun. We tried putting it aside, but that was the problem. We were so worried about keeping things smooth that we never talked about things like that. Simple cookie making. Feeling sad.

So I filled up a big tupperware full of cookies and wrapped a red and green plaid ribbon around it. I'm going to the hospital, Will, I called to him. He didn't answer, I don't even know if he heard me. But when I got in the car, I sat there shivering and wished he would come along. Then I remembered my mother had been on an IV for the past six months. She couldn't eat a thing. She couldn't eat Christmas cookies.

"So why did you fight him?" I ask, waiting. There is no answer. "Matt, answer the question." Snow covers the sidewalk, then melts. My feet are numb.

"I don't really know how to tell you," he says. "You'll be mad."

"So maybe I will be," I say, "but you have to tell me anyway. I love Will. You know that." Matt sniffles; I think he is crying. "Why did you fight him?" I ask again. "That's so dumb. Will wouldn't want to fight anybody."

"I know," Matt says. "But while you were at work, I called him to see if he wanted to go out or something. I think I made him nervous, but he said sure. I think he thought there was something wrong. So I picked him up and we drove all around the country. I had some beer and we drank that. Will kept asking if I needed to talk to him about something. So I finally said, 'Yeah, I do have something to talk about.' I pulled over. That was down by the river. When we got out, I swung at him and missed. He thought I was kidding, so I swung again and hit him, in the stomach. Then he got scared and I hit him about five more times before he could do anything. Then he just fell over. He wasn't bleeding or anything. I thought he was dead. But he kept breathing and that's when I drove off to get you. I was scared, you know?"

"You probably killed him," I say and close my eyes. Matt leaps up, says, "You don't even know, do you, why I did it. You don't even know."

"Matt, I'm taking Will to the hospital now. Stay here, I don't want you to come." I walk stonelike into the house. My emotions have frozen up with the rest of my body. But Matt is still agitated. He wants to tell more, but I don't want to hear it. "Help me carry him to the car," I command.

Inside the house it is warm and I want to stay there and turn on the tv and forget this. I want to prop Will up, make him laugh, shake his hand, move his face. But he breathes lightly and sags in the middle as Matt and I pull him up and drag him out to the car. I don't look at Matt. He gets in the front seat next to me.

"Let me tell you more," he says.

"Let's just be quiet for a while," I say back.

When he was in first grade, Mrs. Hoops thought Matt was slightly retarded. I was in third grade and always getting good grades—a teacher's favorite. I didn't think Matt was retarded, I thought he was acting that way for attention. At home he knew lots of things and watched game shows and knew many of the answers. But in school he wouldn't cooperate. He sat and drew pictures of big tall buildings and fires and big tall giants lifting up the buildings. He didn't have any friends except for me. In high school, he rarely spoke. People didn't know what to make of him.

We were really close until my freshman year. Matt was in seventh grade and always skipped school and swore at teachers. I got exasperated. He embarrassed me and he knew it. I would usually find letters from him in my locker about three times a week. He told me that he was depressed, how he thought about dying all the time. He asked me if I'd run away with him. He would look up travel agencies in the Sunday newspaper and price flights all over the country.

When I was a senior and started going out with Bradley, Matt really hit bottom. I knew he was jealous, but I didn't know how much. Mom told me that he cried when I left with Bradley for the evening. I didn't understand him at all then, I thought he was sick and needed help. I talked to my mother, but she was sick herself and didn't know what to do for him.

Whenever I got home from a date, Matt would still be awake. I'd see the slit of light under his door. When I went in the bathroom to wash up, he'd slip into my bedroom and wait for me, scaring me every time.

"What do you want?" I'd ask.

"Let's talk," he'd say.

"About what? I'm tired."

"Well, I'm lonely and I can't sleep. Can I sleep with you?" I let him sleep with me sometimes, but sometimes I made him sleep on the floor on my braided rug with his own pillow and blankets. I felt bad, him laying there on the hard floor all alone and cold. But it was too strange with him in bed with me. It made me nervous and I'm not sure why. I guess I thought he was too old to be acting that way.

At the hospital they immediately wheel Will out of sight. A nurse takes me by the arm to a little room to fill out the forms on her clipboard. Matt tries to come along, but they make him wait in the waiting room. The nurse is polite, blonde-haired and skinny. She keeps waiting for me to answer.

"Are you?" she asks.

"What?" I say. "I'm sorry."

"His wife? Are you his wife?"

"No, I'm not. We live together." I feel cheap and embarrassed and young. She asks me his full name and date of birth and place of birth and I get scared because I can't remember if I even know. Not even his middle name.

"It's all right," she says. "Just relax." I try to, but my mind keeps flipping to Will and Matt and I feel sick, dizzy. I put my head between my knees. "Are you all right?" she asks, standing up. She puts her arm around my shoulders and tries walking me around. I tell her I'm okay, I just haven't eaten and I'm really tired, but I collapse in midsentence. I feel coolness and lightness, and when I open my eyes I see my mother and she's holding my little baby, Laurel, and I fall back asleep again, so happy.

Although I was only about three years old, I remember holding Matt when he was a little baby. He was born premature and felt as light as a doll in my arms. I sat on the couch and held him carefully while Mom warmed his bottle of formula in the kitchen. I was always afraid he would die because he was so tiny and weak, but Mom said, No, he'll make it just fine if we love him all we can. So I did. I was never jealous of all the attention he got as a small baby. I never felt bad about being forgotten.

One day when Matt was almost one, he got really sick. Mom drove us up to the hospital, said he had gotten pneumonia and might die. That was the day of my birthday, and although I knew Matt was very sick, I was angry that my mom had forgotten. I had to sit in the waiting room for hours and kept falling asleep, waking up to the sound of telephones and elevator bells. Once I woke up on a plastic chair and someone had covered me with soft blankets. I thought it must have been my mother, but soon a nurse came to see how I was doing. *That* day I was jealous, because birthdays are important, but only that day.

Matt looked purple when I saw him bundled in all the white hospital blankets. His eyes looked like they were shrinking back into his head. Mom held onto him, tears dripping off her cheeks onto Matt. When I came into the room, she held out her free arm to me and pulled me close to her.

I didn't forget about you, Hannah, was all she said. Then, when I was leaving, she told me to say a prayer for my little brother. But I didn't know how, I never prayed. But when I got back to the waiting room, I tried. I pinched my eyes shut and folded my hands. Please make Matty better, God. And make Mom not sad. And I don't care, really, that this was my birthday.

I wake up in the hospital. Matt sits by the side of my bed. I am in a hospital bed. I jump up, panicked and confused.

"What's happened to Will?" I ask Matt.

"Just relax a minute," he says and tries to get me to lie down again.

"What's happened to him?"

"Just sit down and I'll tell you," Matt says. I sit in a hard chair opposite him. "Well, I guess he's bleeding internally and he's still not conscious. I'm sorry, Hannah. I didn't mean to hurt him like that. I don't know what got into me." He hangs his head.

"How can you sit there and say that? How can you allow yourself so much leeway?" I walk out of the room. I don't know where Will is, don't know which doctor to ask. They all walk past, looking at their watches and yawning. I walk up to the main desk and tell them my name and ask about Will. They say he is still being watched and that a specialist is going to see him soon. He is bleeding internally. I hold onto the counter. We just have to wait, the nurse says. I stare at her and she shrugs uncomfortably. I tell her to call me if anything happens. She nods.

Matt is waiting at the door for me. I tell him to give me the car keys. He won't. I tell him again. He walks out the door. I feel like vomiting and crying at the same time. I follow him out and try grabbing the keys out of his hand, but he pulls away.

"What are you doing," he says. "You're hysterical." Then he softens, snow melting in his hair and on his face. "Hannah, just come over to Mom's with me. There's nothing else to do right now. Come on. They said he's going to live. Come on."

I walk to the car and stand there in front of the driver's door. "For the last time, Matt, give me the car keys. I need to go think." I hold out my hand.

Matt unlocks the passenger door and gets in. He unlocks my door and opens it. I don't want to, I truly don't, but he wins. I let him. I hold on to everything else, but I get in. I start up the car. It's cold, so it takes a long time. I don't know where I want to go. Wherever I go, Matt will come with me. The thought is both comforting and annoying. What if we do go home, what then? I don't know where to begin. Everything inside me feels old and decayed and I blame Matt. It's his fault. He has reached in and taken all my energy.

"Matt," I say, pulling out of the parking lot, "no one will ever love me like Will does." He nods and looks out the window. He blows hot breath on it to melt the frost. I know Matt loves me, too. Beyond how much a brother normally loves a sister. But sometimes I turn into his mother, so it's confusing. He has no mother. Neither do I. So we lean on each other, we feed off each other for everything. Even Will could not provide what Matt gives me. And yet I hate Matt for it.

I drive to Mom's house on the edge of town. Tall jack pines protect it. The big house is safety for me. Matt gets out and splashes through the snow sludge. I wish our mother were alive and home and would make it better. It feels lonely and even scary as Matt creaks open the wooden door. We stomp our feet on the mat instinctively.

I'm going to confront Matt. I decide as he hangs up his coat that I'm not going to hold anything back. It seems like a strange circular dream back here, as if Will could very well be lying unconscious on our couch again. But he's not. The house is empty and quiet. Matt takes off his boots, shivers with cold. I want to wring his neck, scratch him. I want to hit him as hard as he hit Will. But I say calmly, "Do you want some coffee?"

"Yeah, that would be great."

"Good, I'll make some." And he sits down where Will lay before.

It isn't fair, really, how some people have to lose all the people they love. I mean, my mother first. They found tumors in her throat. We thought that was bad. Then, little by little, they started removing pieces of her actual body. I remember the day they had to slit right down her throat and remove everything. That was the last day she could speak. She didn't say much. I tried to make conversation, but she would only smile and agree. It was uncomfortable.

Matt didn't come that day. He was too weak for things like that. That's what he said. He has always been weak. So, for those weeks afterward, I had to spend time up at the hospital with her, carrying on a monologue about stupid things that happened at work, how Will was doing, how I had cleaned her house. All this just to keep up her morale. Actually, I think she would have liked it better if I hadn't kept up that nervous talking. But how could I really know? Her eyes were dark and sad. Sometimes I would read to her, just to fill up space. She liked Jane Austen. She could read by herself, but it was more for me, gave me something to do. But just like that, she slipped away. It was no surprise. And yet it was. I still feel like she'll be calling me up any day now. It's not fair. Matt makes it even more unfair by being weak. And by taking the only sure thing in my life and making him bleed.

The coffee is done. I hear it drizzling its final drops into the pot. Matt waits in the living room, his arms crossed. I fill two mugs and bring him one. I'm surprisingly upbeat and for a moment it seems almost ludicrous, what I'm going to say. I have to drink almost my whole mug of coffee before I speak.

"Matt, what are you going to do?" I ask.

"What do you mean?"

"When Will is better, when you don't have me to run to?"

"I don't think that far ahead," he answers. He thinks he's gotten past me, thinks he's won me over again. But he hasn't. I have to be honest with him, no matter what the cost.

"Matt, you've got to quit this. You have to stop needing me. I can't take care of you. And you didn't succeed with Will, whatever you were trying to do, it didn't work at all.

So now you've lost me." For a long time Matt says nothing. He taps his feet.

"Can't you forgive me, Hannah? I didn't know what I was doing."

"You didn't know what you were doing? Oh, I see, you didn't know what you were doing." I smile. "It doesn't matter what you say, Matt. Don't you understand? Not everything is indestructible. So, I don't want to see you around anymore, Matt. Really, I don't want to see you ever again." I wonder to myself if I'm lying as I say it, but I look hard into his green eyes and make him believe it. He looks like a boy in a big overgrown bulky body. There's not much more I really feel for him. Maybe pity. Maybe some sense of hopelessness. But I won't give him any more. Underneath my patient talk, I think I'm tearing his face off. I think I'm pushing his head into the pillow until he can't breathe. I'm slapping his face over and over and over. And after my little speech, he just shrugs his shoulders, the cocky little bastard, shrugs his shoulders.

"Whatever you want, Hannah," he says.

But I know, without a doubt, he won't make it without me. He's proven too many times, he can't.

When I was little, I wanted to be a veterinarian. Then we got three cats and one of them, the momma, got cancer on her head and I watched it eat up her body pink. I decided then I could never be a veterinarian. So I would be a teacher. I was a good speller and a good student and I thought I would make a good teacher. But then I saw my favorite teacher, Mr. Graves, hit a misbehaving boy and get fired. Teachers had tough lives, I decided. For a long time I didn't want to be anything.

My mother told me that my father was a carpenter and then he went to be a soldier. I didn't know what a soldier was exactly, but she told me it was someone who had to fight for their country and for freedom. I felt proud and told all my friends that my father was a soldier. They weren't impressed at all. But I was. I wondered if he had died in battle. My mother told me it was no glamorous thing and nothing to be proud of. I asked her if he was dead. She thought for a long time and said she wasn't sure, but she had a gut feeling he was.

But I got excited, thinking that he just might drive up any day and find us. Just pull up in the driveway and pick me up in his arms. I thought things would be better if we had a dad. Matt became obsessed with his return. He said we needed a good man around the house to keep things in order. I thought it would be fun, make us a family.

But as I got older, I stopped looking out the window, stopped expecting anyone to return. We were a threesome and that's what we'd always be. Mom started asking me if I wanted to go to college someday, but I was unsure. Not that I didn't want to go, but it felt like I had to stay around in case something came up. I had to take care of her, take care of Matt. Who would take care of them, after all, but me?

When I was a senior, she asked me what I wanted to be. I said maybe a lawyer, or an obstetrician, because I liked babies. Mom said I would need college for those and I had better start looking, but I still felt that pull to stay around, to be near her. And then I got pregnant. And then my baby died. I thought it would never be too late. And I never dreamed I'd be a waitress with no mother and no baby and so unhappy.

Rollie Wishes

ROLLIE WATCHES it snow from his second-story window. He sits on the warm radiator and fingers the cyst on his face. It sits, tight and round, in the concave of his sinus cavity. Again, he goes to the mirror in his tiny bathroom to examine his profile. He thinks the cyst is the likeness of a small preteen breast—not that big, but the same round blooming effect. Shoulders slouched, he flips off the light and goes to his cluttered desk, where he keeps a record of his financial situation. Since his new job, he has been able to save only fifty dollars, which isn't that bad considering he just started a month ago. Rent takes up most of his money—he pays $300 a month for a big upper duplex on Franklin Avenue. It could be cheaper if he wanted a room-mate, but who would he live with? He doesn't really have that many friends. Besides, he likes the feeling of his own place, his own Mr. Coffee, his own footsteps resounding off the hardwood floors, his own stack of mail in the box. The neighborhood is depressed and run-down—drunk men loiter in front of the bingo hall and soup line, car windshields are shattered, big houses are boarded up — but the street Rollie lives on is quiet and lined with tall shadowy maples, so he feels safe and cozy enough.

According to a doctor he had seen last fall, an operation to remove the cyst would cost around $2,500, including a full day in the hospital to guard against infection. That was more money than Rollie could make in two months. His job at Biovascular (where he sterilizes umbilical cords, sews them together and packs them in long test tubes, his co-workers being four athletic women who were biology majors in college, the lab where he works being out in the farthest suburb in a modern brick building with smoky glass windows) only pays $5.25 an hour. Luckily he has a friend, Rip, (a self-proclaimed nickname) who drives a cherry red Trans Am and lets Rollie ride to and from work with him for free. Rip works in the packaging department, so they don't see each other all day and don't have much to talk about on the rides home. Rollie admires Rip — the way his pants match his shirts perfectly, his apartment building with a heated swimming pool, his snakeskin cowboy boots.

But as far as expenses go, Rollie still can't seem to afford anything extra, not to mention a minor surgical operation. Still, it has been eating at him lately, ever since Kay, one of his co-workers, had said, "Rollie, any girl would break her neck to go out with you if it wasn't for that — " Then she had broken off what she was going to say (which was all too obvious to everyone in the room, all four of them) and had tried to change the subject. It was too late. She asked in a peppy voice if anyone wanted to bet on the Vikings' game Sunday. No one wanted to, and all Rollie could think about was getting rid of the ugly cyst on his face. How could he hide it? Or ever forget about it? It was like having a hole in the armpit of your sweatshirt—always knowing it's there, checking yourself to make sure no one sees it, trying to remember not to raise your arm. There was no way people could even pretend not to see it.

What Rollie really desires lately is a girlfriend. His mother constantly calls him from Lake City and asks him if he has enough money and if he's met any nice girls. Rollie says no every time to every question, but feels sick and sorry about how empty his life must sound to his mother. He compensates by talking animatedly about his job, making it sound lucrative and intense, when it's actually just messing with piles of milky cow arteries. It's a stupid job, as far as Rollie is concerned, but he doesn't tell his mother that. He doesn't really tell her the truth about anything. Why bother?

It's Sunday afternoon, Rollie's most hated day because he has to think about going to work another full week with no highlights or interruptions. The Mr. Coffee drizzles away at its third pot of the day, but Rollie doesn't even know if he'll be able to drink it all, and he hates to waste. He wishes he had a girlfriend who would stay overnight, who'd sleep pressed close to him and drink coffee with him in the morning. Actually he has never officially tried to get dates. It seems contrived to Rollie, when he thinks about getting dressed up and smearing on cologne and planning a movie date. He wishes it would just happen. But what just happens? That's what depresses Rollie—you have to work so hard for everything you want.

He decides to call Rip, even though they rarely associate with each other outside of work. But why not take the chance? Rip knows lots of different people, maybe he could set Rollie up with someone. As he dials, Rollie feels a sudden panic squeeze his chest, and he almost hangs up, but the deep rumble of Rip's voice jolts him.

"Yeah, this is Rip."

"Hi, Rip. This is Rollie. What're you doing?" Rollie thinks his voice sounds weak and flimsy next to Rip's. He clears his throat.

"Watching the game. Aren't you?" There is the muffled sound of tv sportscasters in the background, and Rollie feels even lonelier. He instinctively reaches up to finger the cyst on his cheek, which, again, makes him want to hang up. He wishes he had never called.

"Yeah, I'm watching," Rollie lies. He decides to just dive in. "Rip, I was wondering, you know your girlfriend, Tasha? Does she have any friends that might want to go out with me sometime?" There is rising background noise, and Rollie wonders if Rip would even notice if he hung up.

"Holy shit, Rollie, they intercepted and now it's overtime. I can't believe this." Rollie hears Rip whistle through his teeth. "Sorry about that, I was wrapped up in the game. Now what was that you were saying? About Tasha?"

"Well, I was just wondering if she had any friends that might want to go out with me sometime, you know, like the four of us together?" Rollie wishes he was dead. There is a large silence.

"Hmm, can't think of anybody just offhand. Rollie, this is good to hear! I thought you didn't like girls or something." A click is heard on the line. "Hey, look, I got another call. I'll think on it and talk to you Monday—hey, that's tomorrow already, shit." The beep is heard again. "Gotta go, 'bye." Rollie is disconnected. Again, he wishes he had never called.

He walks into the kitchen and thinks of something to eat. Lately he has been prone to big sausages and various styles of potatoes, usually fried. He sits down at the wobbly card table, covered with sewn-together bandannas that his little sister, Rhonda, made for his last birthday. He cannot see clearly out the window, covered with hazy plastic to keep out the cold, but he knows it has precipitated. Water beads cling to the plastic and jiggle in the wind. His dirty spilled-on kitchen floor is covered with latch-hook rugs his mother made him last Christmas; he tries to cover everything up. Rollie opens a can of Star Label tomato soup and goops it into a tiny dented saucepan. As usual, he is irritated at how poorly the mixture blends with the can of milk he is instructed to add and, so, tries to smash the oily red globs to the side of the pan with the wooden spoon. As the soup is cooking, he finds one-half of a package of saltines, but after putting one in his mouth, finds they are stale. He throws the whole thing into the overflowing trashcan, sighs and winces—a sinus headache. He rubs his oily temples, subconsciously reaches down to caress the cyst on his cheek. The soup bubbles furiously into a pink foam around the edges. Rollie stirs, then jumps when the phone rings. He is afraid to answer it, and waits until the fifth ring.

"Hello?" he answers, expecting the worst.

"Rollie? This is Rip." He waits for some recognition. Rollie is silent. "You'll never guess what, Rol. Tasha's relatives are all in town for some anniversary deal for her grandparents or something stupid like that . . . anyway," Rip stresses the *anyway* like a teacher might do to hold the students' attention, "they're all staying overnight, and Tasha and her cousin Kristine don't have anything to do, so I remembered what you asked me before about going out on some date. So, Tasha and Kristine are going to meet us later at her place. How's that grab you?"

Rollie turns off the soup. "Tonight?"

"Yeah, tonight."

"But it's Sunday. I mean, I didn't mean right away. I have to work tomorrow." Rollie licks the spoon from the tomato soup. Scalded milk shreds stick to the tip and taste like cheese. "I don't think I can make it, Rip."

"You can't say no now, Rollie. It's already settled. Kristine's excited to meet you. She's really pretty if I remember right. Come on."

Rollie feels himself shrinking back. He feels a tingle in his armpits — that nervous indication just before sweating. He thinks of his cyst, how embarrassed the girl will be when she sees it. He wonders if Rip has told her about it, but he is too embarrassed to ask. He thinks he could try to be humorous about it, make light of it, but he hates people like that. "I can't. I just can't."

"Well, then you're going to have to call her back, Rollie, because I'm not going to. You're the one who called me and wanted a date. You wanted one, you got one. So, I'll see you at 8:00."

"All right." Rollie succumbs.

"And don't worry about how you look or anything. Kristine is cool."

"All right. See you later." Rollie hangs up in haste. He pours the soup into a deep ceramic bowl and sits in front of it at the card table. He decides he will have to go through with it. He retrieves the crackers from the garbage and dunks a stack into the bowl, breaking them in half with the tip of his spoon. The break sounds dull and muffled.

When he finishes eating, it is about 7:30. Rip will pick him up very soon, so Rollie goes into his narrow bedroom, mostly taken up with his double bed covered with unzipped, down-filled sleeping bags, and looks in the mirror. He slicks back his dark, even hair with some cream his grandfather gave him years ago. With his hair back, his eyes look more penetrating and, he hopes, become more of a focus than the cyst on his face. He wishes he could wipe away the cyst that seems to be turning a deep red color. To try to look relaxed, he slips on a plain black t-shirt and layers a red-and-black lumberjack shirt over it, with faded Levi's as the base of the outfit. He bunches up a fresh pair of tube socks and sticks his moist feet inside all their softness. He hates to wear sour, day-old socks. So, he is ready, except for brushing his teeth. Back in the bathroom, he spreads the thinnest layer of green Aim over his brush. Who needs to waste? And how much toothpaste actually ends up down the drain anyway? He has good straight teeth; that's one plus. Thinking he hears a car horn, he turns off the faucet, and sure enough, it's Rip, early, on top of everything else. Rollie wipes his mouth with a hand towel and grabs his coat, feeling for keys in the left-hand coat pocket. They're there. He locks the door and runs out to meet Rip in the Trans Am. To Rollie's surprise, it's snowing big wet flakes that melt upon reaching the Trans Am's windshield. Before strapping into his seatbelt, Rollie panics for his wallet, then feels the familiar square in his back pocket and relaxes.

"Rollie—looking good, I must say." Rip has his seat tipped way back, and drinks a Dr. Pepper, which he occasionally sets between his legs. His jeans are the darkest blue, and the glint of a thick gold chain shines from the thicket of chest hair curling out of Rip's half-buttoned plaid shirt.

"What are we going to do tonight?" Rollie asks. He stares out his window at the passing flakes of snow.

"Drink, I suppose. Do you drink?" Rollie nods yes. "I don't know what else. We'll see what happens." Rip crushes the pop can in his fist and throws it in the backseat. "You play pool?" Rollie shakes his head no. "How about darts?" Rollie shrugs, then jumps as Rip slams his fist on the steering wheel. "Damn, it's weird to be hanging out with you and not be going to work! Whoo!" Rip laughs and punches Rollie on the arm. Rollie smiles.

After driving down Franklin Avenue—out of the poor

district and into the uptown area—Rip careens his car into the driveway of a big brick house on Pleasant Avenue. A light goes off in the front room, and two slim figures run out of the house. "Let's get out," Rip suggests. To be gallant, Rollie thinks. All four of them stand in front of the Trans Am. Tasha, a tall brown-haired girl wrapped in a huge royal blue coat, introduces everybody.

"And Kristine, this is Rip's friend, Rollie. They work together at Biovascular. Rollie, this is Kristine." Rollie holds out his hand for a shake. Kristine has big wide eyes and long auburn hair twisted into a braid. Self-consciously, Rollie turns his left side away from her, to hide the cyst. She seems unaffected and calm. Rollie makes way for her as she climbs into the tiny backseat. Rip and Tasha slam their doors in unison, and they are off.

"Who's interested in throwing a few darts?" Rips asks, looking into the rearview mirror. Rollie eeks out an uncertain murmur. He turns to Kristine, his date, and shrugs his shoulders nervously. Rip takes all of this as a yes, and swings his car smoothly into an empty slot outside of the C.C. Club. Inside, the place is crowded and smoky, which irritates Rollie. In a sudden burst of bravery, and beginning to feel a bit more comfortable, he takes Kristine by the elbow and guides her to the inside of a bright red booth, a perfect spot, right by the dartboard. Rollie hasn't played darts since junior high, and begins to doubt his ability, which leads him back to worries about the cyst on his cheek. He feels himself flush. In the meantime, Rip negotiates with the waitress about darts, orders a pitcher of beer and tests the dartboard's scoring, leaving Rollie alone with Tasha and Kristine with nothing to say. He makes an effort. "So, where are you from?" he asks Kristine, the one he feels he should be talking to.

She fiddles with the end of her thick braid, which is shiny, like the end of a brand new paintbrush. "My family is from Kenyon, south. Do you know of it?" Rollie shakes his head as a waitress clunks down a heavy pitcher of beer and four glasses. At the dartboard, Rip pushes buttons and sticks the plastic-tipped darts in and out of the bullseye. Rollie wishes Rip would join them at the table. Kristine startles him as she continues talking.

"I'm just up here visiting my grandparents. I don't usually like the city so much – too big for me. I like a quiet place where I can think." She moves her glass around on the soft tablecloth in circles. Tasha looks bored, and gives Rollie a faint, tired smile as his gaze passes over her.

Rollie feels as if he somehow understands Kristine, since he too hates living in the city. He wants to tell her about growing up on the farm in Lake City, but fears it might be too personal to say just yet. He wonders what she thinks about the boil on his cheek, if she would ever dream of kissing him. Would she? The beer goes down easily, and Rollie finds himself pouring a second glass before the others have even finished one. Rip rejoins them in the booth.

"The damn dartboard doesn't even work. Unless you guys want to play and not keep score?" He gets no response. "Well, then I say we just have a couple pitchers and go somewhere else." Rip reclines way back so it looks as if he is almost lying down. His long cowboy-booted legs jut out into the aisle, and all the waitresses are forced to maneuver around him.

"Just relax for once, Rip." Tasha says. "You don't always have to be doing something, do you?" Rip glares at her and crosses his arms.

"Well, no, but Rollie was the one who wanted to come out and do something fun tonight." Rip snorts, takes a big swig of beer, swishes it around in his mouth, then blows out a silent burp. He looks at Rollie for a retort, but Rollie merely flushes and looks away.

There is a heavy uncomfortable silence, in which Rollie can almost feel the cyst on his face growing, becoming shinier, redder. He feels it sticking out almost as far as his nose, and it makes him freeze inside, terrorized. He feels sick to his stomach. The top of his head tingles and the whole room spins. He tries to swallow, but his mouth is too dry to work properly. His mind races, thinking how stupid he must look to Kristine, how this whole thing must have been a joke, how desperately he wishes he was still at home in his wonderful, quiet apartment. The last thing he remembers hearing is a deep exhausted-sounding sigh from Kristine, then complete silence.

He wakes up confused, dazed and irritated by the light, stinging slaps Rip issues to his cheeks.

"Rollie, Rollie! Wake up! Jesus, what happened to you?" Rip towers over him, surrounded by Kristine and Tasha, and several curious bar patrons.

"I'm okay, it's all right," Rollie staggers to his feet, unclear as to what happened. "I'm sorry. Really, I'm all right." He politely waves away the waitress who is insistent about calling an ambulance. Rollie slouches back into the booth and rubs his temples. He jumps as Kristine touches his forehead. "I'm sorry," he apologizes to her. "I just don't feel well."

Rip looks at his watch and rolls his eyes at Tasha. He wraps his arm around her shoulder, then pulls them both closer to the table to talk quietly to Rollie. "Look, Rollie, do you want to go home? It's okay, just say so."

"What time is it?" Rollie has no reason for asking such a question.

"Almost nine," Rip replies without looking at his watch.

"I think I better go home. If you guys don't mind." In

unison they all say it's all right, and pull on their jackets. Rollie doesn't even try to make conversation anymore, as if his fainting has given him immunity. No one else talks in the car as they wheel down Lowry Hill, back into the poor section of town where Rollie lives. He watches out the window as the buildings become shabbier and more rundown, many of them condemned and boarded up with big pale plywood. They pass four SuperAmerica stores before reaching Rollie's house.

"I'm really, really sorry about this," Rollie apologizes again as Rip's Trans Am idles smoothly, blowing huge gusts of exhaust up into the cold, empty sky. "Kristine, it was nice to meet you." By this time, he has pulled the seatbelt off of himself and is pushing the front seat forward so he can get out as quickly as possible.

"Hey, Rollie, don't worry about it. Maybe it's the flu or something." Rip gives the car some gas.

"Yeah, maybe." Rollie awkwardly grips the open door and shivers from the cold. "Well, 'bye everybody."

Before he can get away, Kristine steps out of the car to face Rollie in the street. To Rollie's surprise, she asks if it's all right if she comes inside with him for a while to talk, maybe have some coffee. Rollie is stunned speechless. He can't understand why she wants to, but after looking helplessly at the car, he shrugs his shoulders and says okay. Kristine looks genuinely pleased by this, and goes to the car to tell her cousin.

"I'm going to stay here a while with Rollie. I'll call when I need a ride." Rollie watches her speak but doesn't hear what she is saying. He watches as clouds of breath come out of her mouth. She is tapping her feet from the cold. She waves as the car zooms off down the street.

Rollie is silent as he unlocks the front door and treads up the stairs to his apartment. He notices dustballs and paper flecks in the corners and feels ashamed for not having once swept the stairs since he's lived here. Kristine silently climbs the stairs behind him.

Rollie swings open the door, expecting to find something inside to explain why this woman is here with him, but there is nothing, not even a hum.

"You live alone?" Kristine asks, hanging her coat on a chair and rubbing her hands together.

"I do," Rollie replies. "I wouldn't have it any other way."

"Really? I wonder if I would like living alone. I think I would." She walks about the apartment, taking in the decor, examining the latch-hook rugs. She follows Rollie into the kitchen.

"You want something to eat?" Rollie still has his coat on and still grips his keys. He opens the refrigerator; they both peer inside.

"We could warm up some apple cider?" Kristine suggests. "Or do you like it better cold?"

"I like it hot." Rollie lifts the big jug out of the refrigerator with his thumb, and as the cold air hits his face, he is reminded again of his cyst. He shudders and glances out of the corner of his eye at Kristine.

He can't figure out why she is here when she doesn't even know him. What does she want?

"Rollie," she says from the card table where she sits, "why do you think you fainted before?" She smooths the bandanna tablecloth with her long fingers. "What happened?"

Rollie feels himself flush and can't think of an answer. He shakes as he pours cider into two mugs. "I don't know. It was so smoky in there, and I was so hot, I guess I just got dizzy."

"Hmm," Kristine crosses her legs and swings her foot knowingly. "I wonder about you."

Rollie sets a large steaming mug in front of her, and she grips it for warmth. He doesn't sit down by her at the table because he can't bear to face her head on. What can he do? He sits down and turns his left side away, but quickly gets up and heads for the living room. He takes off his jacket and kicks off his shoes. He looks at the empty walls, at his dim light in the corner with the stained lampshade. He curses the unmatching bit of furniture and the worn chenille bedspread wrinkled over the couch. He sits, but gets up quickly, remembering Kristine in the kitchen. He thinks about calling Rip but can't think of any reason to do it.

"Rollie," Kristine calls from the kitchen, "what are you doing?"

"Nothing," he answers. "Why don't you come in here? It's warmer."

She does. She looks at everything, takes everything in as she walks. She is beautiful, Rollie notices, with her thick auburn hair and fair skin. She sits beside him on the couch, and turns to face him.

"I hope you're not nervous that I'm here. I mean, we're almost complete strangers." She sips lightly at the cider, then laughs brightly as if she has come up with a good idea. "I suppose you really do wonder what I'm doing here in your place, don't you!" She laughs again, and Rollie weakly smiles, unsure as to what is so funny.

"Well, I was kind of wondering." Rollie holds his mug to his chest.

"I just get so lonely. I mean, sometimes I wish someone would just grab me and kiss me. Just take me. But it doesn't sound right, how I'm saying it. It's not what you think." She pushes at the stack of books on the floor with her feet. "Don't think I'm stupid."

"I don't think you're stupid." Rollie looks at her, surprised. "Why would I think you're stupid?"

"I don't know. It's weird. I mean, when I'm in Minneapolis, and traveling around like this, I don't think right. To me the best thing is having a good solid place to live, where you can always go and nothing changes. You know what I mean?" Rollie nods. "Can I take off my boots?"

"Sure," Rollie says, gesturing that he has already taken his own off.

Kristine removes her boots and sets them by the radiator, then returns to her previous position beside Rollie. "I just hate not having a real place right now. First I lived in Kenyon, then I moved up here for a while, worked a bunch of weird jobs and went out with a fry cook, then I thought about marrying him, then I moved back to Kenyon and sat around with my parents, and now I don't really know what I want to do." She sets her feet on the big trunk Rollie uses as a coffee table. "I get so lonely for a friend."

Rollie feels like he should respond somehow, but how? Is she coming on to him? It doesn't seem like it. He has never kissed a woman in all his twenty-nine years. Is that what she wants?

Kristine sighs loudly. "I bet you feel embarrassed about the bump on your face, don't you?" She doesn't look at him as she asks the question. Rollie feels a freeze, a sting pass through his entire body. He feels it deep in the nugget of the cyst on his face. He feels it pushing and pulsating at the tip of the cyst. He feels like vomiting. "I bet that's why you passed out at the bar," Kristine continues, "because Rip just set you up and you didn't even want to come probably, right?"

Rollie tries to swallow. He takes a deep breath and looks into her eyes. "What do you want?" he asks her.

She meets his gaze. "What do I want? Nothing, Rollie. I just like a little company every now and then." She places her empty mug on the trunk. "I already told you what I want. What do you want?" She starts to lean back on the arm of the couch, then sits up. "Rollie, can I lean against you? Can I put my head here?" She rests her head on

Rollie's shoulder and breathes deeply. "Ahh," she sighs. Rollie remains rigid, then relaxes. He likes the feeling of her head on his arm, her warm hair. He can't think of anything to say. Her breathing sounds as if she is almost asleep. He does not move a muscle. Suddenly, he feels her hands reaching up to his face. Her fingers lightly rest on his lips, they finger his jawline, outline his nose. His chest begins heaving as her fingertips carefully touch the curve of his cyst. He stiffens; his breathing shallows. With the pads of her fingers, she lightly rubs it, massages it. Then, she lets her hand drop lightly on his chest. She turns his face to look at her.

"It's okay, Rollie. Don't you see? Won't you kiss me now?" Rollie is confused by the urgency in her deep green eyes. He himself touches the cyst, grimacing. He cannot kiss her, but he will hold her.

Rudy and Bette's New Year

BETTE

I'm standing in the bathroom with one leg in the sink when Rudy comes in with his soap and towel and after-shave. "Bette," he says, "what are you doing in here?" He doesn't even look to see that I'm shaving my legs. "I'm shaving my legs," I say, not looking up. If I would've known beforehand how rude Rudy was, I never would've married him. He assumes too much, takes up too much space. At restaurants, he orders before me. In the car, he turns the radio up full blast when he knows I hate the radio. I could go on forever.

Tonight we're going to a New Year's Eve party at our friend Faye's. Actually, I met Faye through Rudy. She got married to his best friend, Sean Walker, who died of a heart attack about three years ago. They've always had the New Year's Eve party at their house. Rudy doesn't like to go since Sean died, but it's about the only time we have to get together with our old friends. So, I talk him into it. It's usually fun. *I* love it, but then I've always been more of a socialite than Rudy. I bought a new outfit for the party. It's a black dress with metallic gold sleeves. Rudy said it's too glitzy, that nobody gets that dressed up, but that's exactly my point. I've got to liven things up around here. All our friends are terribly Minnesotan. They're too conservative. I was born and raised right outside of Manhattan, so when I came out here for college and met Rudy, it was quite a change.

"Rudy, what time is it?" I yell. He doesn't answer. I run out of the bathroom with wet legs and feet and see Rudy lying on our bed, asleep. "Are you sleeping, honey? Come on, wake up, we've got to get going."

RUDY

I'm not really sleeping, I'm faking. I don't want to go to the New Year's Eve party. Every year we go through this—I want to stay home with the kids, Bette wants to go and get drunk at Faye's. She thinks I don't want to go because of Sean, and that's partially true, but mostly I hate to sit there while all the men hit on Bette. She loves it, I know she does. And she's not really doing anything wrong, so I can't say anything.

"I'm awake," I say to Bette as she pulls on her black nylons. Her legs are long and muscular. "You look great," I tell her. "Come here." I pull her face over to mine and try to kiss her, but she resists.

"I just put lipstick on," she says, and picks up her high heels. "You don't want to go, do you?" She sits on the edge of the bed and buckles the thin straps around her ankles.

"I do, I'm just tired." Actually, I don't. I hate New Year's Eve and I always have. It used to be because of the hangovers, but now I'm dry. I haven't had a drink in over six years. I've been going to AA and that helps me out, but this New Year's Eve stuff gets to me. Bette drinks. She didn't at first, to help me get through, but now she sees no reason why she shouldn't. She doesn't have a problem, after all. So she says. I don't know. She drinks a lot. And for some reason, all the men at these parties think it's perfectly okay to touch Bette and kiss her, as if I don't care. Bette says I'm too shy, that I need to open up a little. When midnight hits, I step outside for a cigarette because I'm not the kind of person to run around the room kissing everyone. Maybe I am a different person now that I'm sober—more serious. But when Bette walks out of the room with a guy, I don't know what to think. I know she'd never cheat on me, it's the guys I don't trust. Bette's gorgeous. Everyone knows it. She knows it, but it suits her somehow. I just can't decide if she's trustworthy.

"Bette, come on, it's my turn to use the bathroom," I say. She sticks her head out of the doorway, blow-drying her hair. "What?" she yells.

BETTE

Faye lets us in. She looks tired already. "I thought you forgot or something. Where have you been?" She takes our coats, squeezes them in between the others in the closet.

"Oh, we had to bring the kids over to Rudy's mom and dad's and Rebecca was coughing so hard I thought she had pneumonia or something, so we stayed there for a while to see if she was all right. She's sleeping now." I smooth my dress and hair and Rudy immediately slips his arm around my waist and pulls me near him.

"How are you, Rudy?" Faye asks.

"Pretty good," he answers, looking at me.

Faye knows what I like to drink. She runs off and comes back with a goblet of red wine. "Rudy, there's some pop or some nonalcoholic punch. What would you like?" Faye always makes sure to have something Rudy can drink.

"Do you have any coffee?"

"Rudy," I interrupt, "don't be impolite. Here Faye went to all this trouble, the least you can do is take what she's offering."

"Oh, Bette, it's no bother. Of course there's coffee. Come on in the kitchen." Rudy follows her and I walk into the pack of people. I hate being owned by Rudy at parties. He always has to make it known to everyone that I'm his. We've been married almost ten years now, you'd think he'd stop worrying.

"Mark, hi."

He looks around and walks over to me. Mark works with Rudy at the architecture firm. "How are you, Bette?" He holds an empty glass.

"I'm all right," I say.

"Where's Rudy?" Mark takes one last sip out of his glass.

"He's getting something to drink."

"Boy, you really look great tonight. Turn around once." I hesitate, then turn. Mark whistles. "Pretty good." I smile and thank him. "I love your accent. It doesn't seem to go away, does it? You're a New Yorker at heart. You know, I lived in New York for a while. I hated it. Too fast for me."

"Really," I say, watching Rudy across the room. He sits by himself, drinking coffee from a mug. On New Year's Eve.

"Do you want some more wine?" I nod. Mark puts his arm around me and we walk to the bar Faye has set up at the other end of the living room. Mark refills my glass with wine and pours himself some vodka on the rocks. Mark is getting old and shows it. His hair is completely gray, but it becomes him. I keep an eye on Rudy. Faye is crouched next to his chair, talking to him. "Just a minute," I say to Mark, who is telling me about his trip to Las Vegas, "I have to go do something."

"I'll be right here," he calls after me.

RUDY

I talk to Faye out of one side of my face. I've been watching Bette. Bette and Mark. I think Faye keeps talking to me because she knows how I get at these parties, unlike Bette who livens up, turns into a different person. I think she's bored with me, we don't even disagree about anything anymore. As she talks to Mark, I can see almost all of her bare back. The dress plunges down in a V and rests on the edges of her shoulders. I wish I could go touch her, her smooth skin.

Faye touches me on the shoulder and I barely notice as she leaves. I watch how the words come out of Bette's mouth, how her lips shine, how one leg bows into the other as she stands. I hope she's happy, though I doubt she really is. Bette wanted to be an actress. She went to college for it, even went on to graduate school, but she never finished, never tried. Now we have enough money. We have three kids. But it seems like Bette wants more than I can give. That's why I hate these parties. It seems like she's looking for the missing piece.

I think Bette is drunk, but I'm not sure. She nods at everything Mark says. Faye walks around the house, giving everyone noisemakers and hats. It's almost midnight. Faye pushes a pointy silver hat onto my head and stretches the string under my chin. "Now, don't leave," she says, pointing at me. It isn't worth it to leave anyway. I don't care what happens. It bothers me that I don't care, but I don't. For a minute I'm tempted to have a beer. Just one. I can taste the chill and bubble running down my throat, the sting. But AA has won me over. Whenever we feel this way, we're supposed to call our sponsors, no matter where we are or when. Bruce Barnett is my sponsor, but I won't call him. I can do this. I've done it before.

While I'm thinking of all of this, Bette comes and sits in my lap. "How are you doing, Rudy?" She smells like booze, not surprising, but I wish she didn't. Her eyes are red and bleary around her contacts.

"I'm all right."

"It's almost midnight."

"I know," I say, and lean my head on her. Just then Faye motions to us that we have a phone call. I tell Bette to get off, and I answer it in the kitchen.

"Who was that?" Bette asks me back in the living room.

"That was Mom. She said Rebecca's really sick and is crying for you. She threw up a couple times."

"Oh, no." Bette hangs onto the doorway. She can't quite stand up straight without tipping a little.

"Well, we better go get her or something," I say, angry at Bette for being so unhelpful.

"Yeah," Bette says, "let's go get her." It takes Bette a long time to say good-bye. I stand at the front door with the keys in my hand, coat on. I hold out Bette's coat for her, but she shakes her head, she's too hot.

Inside the car, Bette leans way over and holds herself. Now she is cold and I put her coat around her. I let the car warm up for a while before pulling out of the driveway. We don't talk. About two blocks away, Bette waves her hands, tells me to stop. "What's the matter?" I say. I pull the car over and Bette throws open her door, sounds like she's choking to death on her vomit. I let the car run, keep it warm. Bette is done, but won't close her door. "Come on, Bette, we have to get Rebecca."

She is shaking with cold. I have no sympathy, no pity. She slams the door shut and lays her head back against the headrest. "You're a good husband, Rudy." She puts her hand on my knee and sighs. I sigh also. Another New Year's Eve over and done.

Hired Hand

"HARLAN, I CAN'T take it anymore. We have to move." Jean leans her forehead against the cloudy windowpane and stares at the dense, green cornfields below. The tassels shake and blow in the wind. She is seventeen years old, nine months pregnant and just married. "I hate it here, Harl." She sighs loudly, then goes to where he sits on the bed, her large belly in his face. She cups her hands around his thick, sunburned neck. "I love you."

Harlan slaps his hands on his knees and shakes his head. "Jean, you've got to have that baby before we can go anywhere." Harlan is a large, tall man, though only eighteen years old. Heavy black hair hangs in his eyes. He and Jean first met at the Ten Pin Bowling Alley a little over a year ago. He saw her sitting with her girlfriends, sipping a Coke, so skinny, such tiny hands that held the pink straw. They fell in love quickly, and the next thing they knew, Jean had become pregnant. "If we move, where are we going to put the baby? And just where would we move to?" Harlan scratches his head with a thumbnail.

Jean and Harlan live on the second floor of a big farm-house in Elwood — the Heisel family's — an old German clan with eight kids, 150 holstein cows and about 200 acres of sweet corn. Harlan milks the cows every morning at 4:30 sharp and every evening at 5:00. This he does cheerfully, without fail. In between, he turns golden brown under the sun while he plows the fields, plants the seed, prunes the crabapple trees, mows the lawn, pulls weeds in the garden, fixes broken machinery, runs to the hardware store and does just about everything else Bobby Heisel asks him to do. "You're the best help I've had yet," Bobby had told Harlan the day prior. "All the other sons of bitches are out for a free lunch." Harlan had felt proud, straightened up a bit as he worked.

But Jean is unhappy. Harlan receives his pay, though quite meager, for the work he does on the farm; these are wages he's entitled to. In exchange for free room and board, Jean is supposed to lend a hand around the house — cooking, cleaning, minding the children, washing clothes. But Jean doesn't get along with Bobby's wife, Marge, so she shirks her duties. All day she sits up in her and Harlan's room, reading baby books, newspapers, musty paper-backs from boxes in the barn. On top of everything else, Jean's pregnancy makes her irritable, miserable, too needy of Harlan's attention, and she hates herself for it.

Now Jean paces the room, fingering her nightgown hanging off the door, her books stacked next to the bed, the cool radiator, Harlan's wallet on the bureau. "I just feel so funny, Harl, like it isn't my house, so what am I supposed to do?"

"I know," Harlan mutters.

Their room is painted warm yellow with high ceilings, wooden floors. They have a small brass bed in the corner, a large bureau with a beveled mirror, an old cranberry-colored sofa and a table with one green plant on it. The curtains are thin, dirty nylon, and wilt in the heat. Suddenly they hear the loud bell clanking back and forth in the kitchen, signaling supper. Outside the sky pinkens and a hot breeze lifts the curtains. Jean sets her hands on her hips, arches her back, rolls her neck in circles, then exhales slowly through her mouth. She lets her hands fall to her sides. "What do they think we are, animals? Imagine ringing a bell at us like that." Jean watches as Harlan undoes his overall straps and stands in boxer shorts and holey black stockings. "I'd sure like to wear short pants down to dinner one of these nights." He pulls on green pleated trousers. "It's so damn hot a guy's like to keel over. Whew." He wipes dirty, oily perspiration off his face. "Come on, sweetie."

Jean starts to speak, then hesitates. She flops down on the bed and bursts into tears. "Did you know I always wanted to be a nurse, Harlan, ever since I was seven? That's what I really wanted." She turns over on her back and squeezes shut her eyes.

"Sweetie, what's the matter with you? Are you crying because you wanted to be a nurse?" Harlan stands beside her and rubs her shoulder. She cries harder. Marge hollers up the stairs that supper is going to get cold. "Be there in a second!" Harlan hollers back. He sits helplessly beside his new wife on the bed. "Now tell me what it is."

Jean's chestnut hair lies in waves across the large pillow. Her green eyes well with tears. "Oh Harlan," she grabs at his collar, "what are we going to do? Why is it like this? I don't know how to have a baby! Help me. Help me, Harlan. Hold me." She grips him tightly and pulls him down beside her on the bed. "We haven't got any money! How am I going to have this baby in a hospital if we have no money?" She lies back on the bed and kicks her feet. "It just isn't fair, Harl, it's not fair. Why does it have to be so hard?"

Harlan slicks his hair back between his fingers. "Now, sweetie, I'm going to take care of it. Didn't I promise I would? I'll talk to Dad tomorrow, all right? Don't worry so much." He grabs her hand and squeezes it, kisses it, then puts a hand to his own stomach. "But I have to tell you, Jean, I'm so goddamned hungry right now I could eat a horse. Now, let's go eat, okay?" Jean nods, sits up. "Good. I love you, you know." He smiles and helps her up from the bed.

Downstairs, the kitchen is humid and steamy with the smell of greasy meat. Gnawed-up corncobs are stacked all over the plates and the kids sit picking their teeth. Bobby and Marge Heisel sit at opposite ends of the table, also picking their teeth between sips of coffee.

"Well, sit down and eat. It's already cold, and if you'd had waited any longer these kids might have eaten it all up on you." Marge laughs as she says this, and looks at the children for a response, but there is none.

At the end of the table, Harlan and Jean sit at the two empty chairs. They ceremoniously say a silent grace, then Harlan grabs two bright yellow cobs out of the dented kettle with his fingers. One he sets on Jean's plate. Self-consciously, they help themselves to milk and bread and the two lone pork chops left on the platter. All the children watch, giggle, then slowly filter out to the front porch.

"Corn's a little chewy and old this time of year," Bobby Heisel breaks the silence. "God, but that young stuff was good around early August, huh, Marge?" She nods, languidly sips her coffee and glances at Jean, who is sliding squares of butter over the golden cob.

"Jean, darling, you look ill. Are you feeling all right? Marge leans over on her elbows. She is big-boned, has large drooping breasts, broad shoulders and a round pale face that scowls. There is a space between each of her teeth. "Are you ready to have that baby yet?"

Jean's mouth is full of food, so Harlan answers for her cheerfully. "She sure is ready. Today's the due date, September second. Jean's been on a crying jag, so I'd bet there's a baby coming soon. Just wait," Harlan says, and gestures with his fork. "It's going to be a boy, too." He soaks up the butter and pork grease on his plate with one last piece of bread, then leans back to rub his belly. "That was damn good, Marge. Thank you."

Marge folds her hands under her chin and smiles. "Now, I'm going to do the dishes, and if it's not too much trouble, Jean, do you think you could give me a hand?" Jean looks up, startled, then turns to Harlan for support.

"Jean needs some rest, you see, so why don't I just give you a hand," Harlan says. Marge smirks. Harlan stacks the plates and loads all the cobs on the big platter when suddenly Jean starts crying and runs out of the room. "Just let her go," Harlan explains, stacking plates. "She'll be all right." He brings all the plates to the kitchen as Marge fills the sink up with sudsy water. Harlan brings in the butter plate, the milk, the salt and pepper, the pork bones, the empty glasses, and sets them on the counter. "Anything else I can help you with?" he says, rubbing his moist hands on his trousers. Marge shakes her head and purses her lips. "All right, then," Harlan says awkwardly, and heads out to the front porch. He finds the whole family there, except Marge, and they are all in the center of the yard, pointing over to the west.

Bobby calls him over. "We've got a funnel cloud coming at us. Look at the sky over there—it's almost yellowish. Doesn't look good."

"No, it doesn't," Harlan replies, and stands with his arms crossed, gazing at the cloud. He holds a hand up. "It's damn still, too, the way a tornado starts."

Bobby shoos the kids back onto the front porch and walks around the house with Harlan. "Well, you know, we've always got the cellar to go into if it comes at us." He stomps his booted foot on the weathered wooden door. "Of course, I'm not scared of a tornado. It's just the animals that they bother. Damned if they don't get fussy."

"Yeah?" Harlan asks.

"Say listen, how about a smoke? I'd like to talk to you about something." Bobby leads Harlan onto the porch, the side where the children aren't. The porch is huge, wraps itself around the big white house like a horseshoe. They sit across from each other on a wooden swing. Bobby produces a tiny pouch of tobacco from his shirt pocket, rolls two wrinkled cigarettes, gives one to Harlan, who wets it with his lips. Bobby lights it, after lighting his own.

"So how's everything with you and Jean?" Bobby asks, propping his feet up next to Harlan.

"All right, I suppose," Harlan answers, dropping ashes onto the floor. "Jean's a little touchy these days, but I'm sure you understand, being pregnant and all."

"Uh-huh. Well, listen, see, our girl Darla, the second oldest?" Bobby ashes his cigarette on the porch floor. "She just wrote telling us she and her husband'll be moving back here. I guess he's out of work or something. Anyway, they've got a little one, too," Bobby sits up straight, then rests his elbows on his knees. "I just don't know any good way to tell you this, but we need that room back for Darla. And of course her husband'll be helping out here on the farm . . . so I hope you and Jean can work something out." He falls silent awhile and gives Harlan time to think.

Harlan says nothing but takes a long drag off his cigarette. "When is Darla due back here?"

"About a week, I think she said."

"Well, it looks like I'm going to have to move fast," is all Harlan says. He smashes the cigarette out with his foot and rubs his hands together. "I just hope our baby can wait awhile."

"I'm real sorry about this, Harlan, you know I am. If it was up to me, I'd have you all stay here with us. But you know how Marge is."

"Yeah, well I better go talk to Jean." Harlan excuses himself and lets the screen door slam behind him as he takes the stairs by twos to their bedroom. Jean stands by the window, chewing her fingernails. She turns to face him. "Harl, look, I think a tornado's coming." They stand with their arms around each other and watch as the black cone twirls its way toward the big house, seeming to head straight for their very bedroom window.

Just then someone hollers up the steps, "Harl! Jean! Get down here in the cellar! There's a tornado coming at us!" They hear the sound of panicked feet pounding down the stairs and rush out of the room, following.

Marge is crouched in the southwest corner of the cellar, holding candles and trying to get a weather station on a small radio. It is all static. The kids crouch down also, looking up at the long rows of canned peaches, pears, jars of stewed tomatoes, withered pickles.

Harlan and Jean crouch down beside each other and wait. "What if we die?" Jean whispers. "Shh," Harlan says, and puts a hand around her shoulder. "What if I have my baby?" Jean whispers again. Harlan shakes his head.

The cellar is dark and damp, and the room they are hiding in is packed tight with six of the children, Marge, Harlan and Jean. Suddenly, there is rumbling heard overhead. The sound of booming, then tearing metal, blowing chunks of wood. The dogs bark and howl.

Bobby Heisel comes down and sits beside the rest, looking pale and out of breath.

"Part of the barn just went," he whispers, then bows his head helplessly.

"Dear Jesus," cries Marge and looks upward for help. The dogs begin to howl again, and then there is silence.

"Oh Harlan," Jean cries, "I think I'm going into labor." She grabs at her protruding stomach and exhales loudly.

Marge hoists herself up and brushes off her pants legs. "I think you'd know if you were in labor, darling." By this time Bobby Heisel is already out of the basement and exploring the damage outdoors. The children linger in the cellar, not willing to let go of the excitement. Marge hollers, "Well, get up you! You better go see if your father needs a hand. Sal, Gordie, go on!" The lanky older boys unfold their limbs and climb up the cellar stairs and out into the open sky.

Harlan lingers over Jean. "Are you sure you're okay, sweetie?" She nods, swallowing back fear, then attempts to rise. "Here, give me your hand." Harlan hoists Jean up into standing position. Marge stands by, gathering her radio, wrapping its cord in tiny circles, smirking at the two of them.

She turns to Harlan. "Did Bobby tell you yet?" She rests the radio on her hip and raises her eyebrows.

"Tell us what?" Jean asks. Her big green eyes widen with curiosity. "Harlan?" All three ascend the stairs. In the entryway, Harlan motions Jean back as Marge pushes past them to the mess outside. "Sweetie," he says, "it looks like we'll be moving after all, just like you wanted."

Jean leans back against the flannel shirts and dirty jackets hanging off the wall. She crosses her arms, and tears glisten in her eyes. "What's going on, Harlan? I never know what's going on around here. Tell me, Harl."

"Bobby just told me on the porch that his daughter Darla's coming back home with her family and they'll need our room. That's what he said." Harlan fishes in his pockets and produces a balled-up Kleenex. "Here," he says. Jean throws it on the floor. "Well, what about this?" She throws her hands around her large stomach. "Well, Harlan," she continues in a high-pitched voice, "What are we going to do? I can't take it anymore."

"It's okay, sweetie," Harlan soothes, pulling her close to him. Suddenly Bobby bursts through the door. Jean and Harlan jump away from each other, startled. "Harl, come out here quick. One of the cows seems to be electrocuted or something. It bolted right into Sal and knocked him over." Bobby's face is bright red and his work shirt disheveled. "Excuse me for a second, Jean. Are you all right?" Jean nods. "Well, come on, Harl. I can't seem to get the damn thing penned up or anything, and I'm afraid it's going to hurt itself."

Harlan shrugs his shoulders at Jean and slips out behind Bobby. Jean follows, lagging behind.

The sky is dark gray and rain clouds hover over to the east. The Heisel children are gathered around the fence just off the side of the barn. They watch tentatively as a large cow charges in haphazard circles, kicking, snorting, rubbing its face in the dirt. Marge tends to Sal in the yard. She peels back his long pants to reveal a purplish crescent-shaped welt on his calf. He bites his lip as she prods the wound with her fingers.

Jean searches for Harlan, who is nowhere to be seen. With the other children, she leans against the wooden fence and resumes watching the agitated cow dart around in the dirt. Shards of torn metal are scattered about the lawn. One side of the barn, freshly painted deep red just this past summer, now shows a gaping, jagged tear, exposing the dark rotting interior where the milking machine is housed.

Jean turns back to the cow, then spots Harlan inside the pen with it. "Harlan," she shouts, "be careful!" He waves a hand that he's heard. Jean bounces up and down nervously as Harlan tries to coax the cow to his side while Bobby waits in the opposite corner with a large bulky rope formed like a noose. The cow kicks and jumps like a rodeo horse. Harlan teases it with a long metal prod which he taps on the cow's rear. A long pink gash is visible on its bony lower leg.

"Jean, run!" Harlan shouts at Jean, but it is too late. Jean and the two smallest children are thrown to the ground as the cow rips through the fence in front of them. After its escape, the cow circles the house, then gallops off into the slim strip of trees beyond the barn.

Harlan gasps as he lifts Jean in his arms. She is limp and mumbles about taking care of the baby. The cow has hit her directly, only after knocking over the two small children, who are apparently uninjured, but stand near by, stunned, rubbing their elbows.

"Jean, where are you hurt? How's the baby?" Harlan asks.

Marge comes running from the front yard, "Well, my God, let's get her inside. Bobby, why don't you get a gun from the basement and shoot that goddamned cow before we're all dead! Come on, let me help you with Jean." Marge grabs Jean under the armpits and bosses Harlan to help with her legs, but Jean is still conscious and fights them both off.

"I'm okay, I'm okay." She stands up, and although a bit shaky, she is all right. "It's a good thing I am okay so I can get off of this damn farm, Marge. You, you witch!" Jean shouts.

Marge stands shocked and hurt, then storms into the house. Harlan and Jean are left standing alone, and Jean picks at the bloody scratches on the palms of her hands. "What did Bobby tell you before?" Jean doesn't look up. "It was Marge, wasn't it? She's the one who wants us to move. I don't believe their daughter is moving back here for one minute." She crosses her arms above her large stomach and glares into the dirt. "Do you?"

Harlan is gazing around the yard at all the damage done by the tornado. Jean exhausts him, the farm work exhausts him, now the tornado has exhausted him. "I'm sorry, sweetie, what did you say?"

"You don't even listen to me! You're like everybody! You think everything is always great! I hate that. I hate everyone! You just stand here and think of all the ways you can help Bobby Heisel when he wants us gone. I hate you!" She starts to cry, tears dribbling into her mouth as she talks. "I could just stand here and have this stupid baby right now and you couldn't care less! Oh, you're so plain!" Jean starts for the house, then deciding against it, she climbs into Bobby's old Cutlass, pushes the seat far back to accommodate her pregnant stomach, feels around for the keys and starts the engine. Harlan is picking up scraps of debris and metal from the yard when Jean yells, "Are you coming with me?"

Harlan looks up. "Coming with you where?" She guns the engine of the dust-coated maroon car, the door still open.

"To your dad's."

"My dad's? What for?" Harlan walks over to the car, then checks over toward the house to see if Marge is around. Jean has never used their vehicles without asking. Even when she does want to use one, she makes Harlan ask.

"I'm moving there. I hate it here, Harlan. I really hate it." She fingers the steering wheel and rests her head on it. "Do you want to join me? Come on."

Harlan keeps looking back at the house. "Jean, just turn off the car. It's going to be okay. Dad's got enough problems over at their place. Come on, sweetie. Turn off the car and we can go take a nap, okay?" He leans his head into the car and reaches for her hand.

Jean starts to cry. "I can't turn it off, Harlan. Don't you understand? I want you to come with me. But you're too good."

"Sweetie, I think you're just having a hard time right now, so maybe you just need to take a nap. Come on. I'll be inside. Okay, sweetie?"

When she doesn't answer, he turns and walks back to the house. Jean revs the engine a couple of times, then turns off the ignition and listens to the silence.

Trailer Court Days

A BARBERSHOP AND 7-UPS

Dad used to have a barbershop in Prospect, Minnesota — a tiny town that only had a grocery store, three bars, a lumber mill and a secondhand junk shop. His barbershop was attached to JoJo's Bar. I loved visiting him in the shop, with the tiny flecks of old men's hair coating the floor — black and gray and white mixed like a powder. Dad would take the vacuum he used for cleaning his customers' necks and tickle my stomach and feet and make it suck at my cheeks. I thought it was hysterical. Then I'd sit tall in the brown padded porcelain chair, my little sister, Rosie, pumping it up high and spinning me around. Sometimes I spun too long and became nauseated. Then Dad would step out to the adjoining bar and buy me a can of 7-Up. But it would take him a long time.

"I'm going to get you some 7-Up, Lizzie. You and Rosie just stay here and if someone comes in while I'm gone, come and get me." He'd be out the door without a backward glance.

I was around nine and Rosie was about six. No one ever came in. We played beauty shop, me spraying Rosie's thin blonde hair down with a mister bottle, slowly wrapping a long thin piece of tissue around her neck, like I'd seen Dad do. I'd snap a black plastic wrap around that, and there she sat in the big chair, hair dark with water, me combing it down in tiny stripes. Then I'd pretend to cut it and ask her what kind of style she was interested in.

One day while Dad was getting me a 7-Up in the bar, and I was spinning Rosie around in the chair, her thin ponytails flying in a blur, an old man walked in with soft gray hair only on the bottom half of his head.

"Is your father around?" he asked, placing his cane carefully on a branch of the coatrack. He shuffled over to a wooden chair for waiting.

"Umm, he's just getting me a pop. I can go get him. He's right next door, in JoJo's," I offered, watching the man in the mirror.

"Well, no, honey, that's all right then . . . I can come back later, or maybe even tomorrow. Say, does your mother know you're here?" he asked, leaning forward in the chair, squinting his eyes.

"Oh, she said we could be here just for a little while," I said, pumping the chair down for Rosie.

"Well, all righty then. You kids be careful." He picked up his cane and stuck it under his arm as he walked out the door.

Then it was my turn to get a haircut, but by that time Rosie was sick from spinning, too.

GRAVEYARD

We used to live in a blue and white trailer, parked down at the edge of town. Everything was so thin in it, so weak, like a lie.

Rosie and I shared a bedroom way down at the end of the hallway. In the afternoons, deep orange sunsets came seeping through the windows. Mostly it was dreary though, paneled with a dark simulated wood like all the other rooms. The walls were so thin they'd cave in if you leaned hard enough. The carpeting was speckled mustard shag—matted and stained from so much playing. You could feel the hollow emptiness of our door when you closed it, so light, with a fake gold-plated knob that didn't lock.

Rosie and I had a huge white cast-iron bed, but it was chipped and showed green and black paint underneath. Once I tried painting over the chipped spots with the white from my watercolor set, but it made it look worse. It was a beautiful bed, though, with intricate iron swirls, loops, dips and curves making up the headboard.

Above our bed was a window that overlooked the Prospect Public Cemetery. When we went to bed at night, we'd stand in our matching flannel nightgowns and look out at the gravestones. Rosie was scared because I told her all the dead people's souls were still alive and were watching us. She'd cry, then we'd jump down into bed and she'd cling to me all night in hot sweaty sleep. I was scared, too.

Other nights we'd lay in bed and giggle, even after Mom had told us through clenched teeth to be quiet. Finally, we'd hear Dad's heavy footsteps pounding down the hall, the sound of his belt unbuckling. He'd slowly open the door, letting a sharp angle of light in, and stand there for a while, tall and silent, slapping the folded leather belt in his palm.

"You girls going to be quiet now?" he'd say, voice gravelly and serious.

We wouldn't say a word. "All right then," he'd murmur, closing the door gently behind him, not shutting it all the way.

I knew he would never hit us, even when he was so drunk the alcohol from his breath filled up our room. But Rosie and I would lie there perfectly still after he left, barely breathing. Then pretty soon I'd feel Rosie's chest fall steady and slow to sleep, while I lay curled up, pressed against the small of her back, eyes still wide open in the dark room.

GLASSES

One night in the trailer we were playing G.I. Joes and Barbies. We were in my older brother Ricky's room, me on the top bunk, throwing Barbies down into a pool we'd made with a mixing bowl full of water. I got tired of going up and down the bunk bed to retrieve the wet dolls, so I jumped right off the bed. I heard a terrible crunch under my knees. I got up and saw what I had done. There were Ricky's taped together wire-rimmed glasses broken beyond repair—small glass squares shattered, but holding together. Ricky was partially blind in one eye and couldn't see a thing without his glasses. He just looked at me, without being mad or anything. Just then Mom poked her head in the doorway, wondering why it had become so quiet. Then she saw the glasses and my sad, guilty face.

"Jesus Christ, Lizzie, you know we can't afford to get Ricky new glasses. What were you screwing around for, huh?" She threw her hands up in the air. "Oh, Lizzie, what are we gonna do?" Then she left the room, leaving Ricky and me alone with the Barbies and the big bowl of water.

WAITING

The red and blue neon signs from Mac's Bar flashed on and off my mother's face as she sat in the front seat of the car, staring straight ahead. Ricky, Rosie and I huddled in the backseat, sleeping restlessly on each other. Most of the time it was too hot for sleep—the bumpy vinyl seats stuck to our little faces. On and off, on and off, the lights flashed in our mother's face and she didn't say a word. Sometimes I would lean over the front seat and look at her, and find a thin, wet tear on her face. But it didn't seem like a sad tear, just tired and hopeless.

Dad just finished playing softball at a tournament like so many others—something about winning the beer trophy. We were all sunburnt and weary from the long day of watching softball games from a big hill—people we didn't even know. Finally, after the sun had gone down and the games were over, we walked over to Mac's Bar. Mac and Janet Hanson owned it, sponsored the team my dad played for, so they knew us. Mac was graying and had tiny slit-blue eyes and looked like a pig with pink pushed-up nostrils. Janet had dark octagonal glasses and a deep red curly perm sprayed tight to her head. They liked us—the Eppler kids! they called out when we came in with Mom and Dad.

Mac's was dim and had a long, glossy wooden bar on one side, deep intimate booths on the other. In the back was a pinball machine and the bathrooms, doors of knotty pine. There were some long tables back there where the families of Dad's team would sit. I drank a lot of Dr. Pepper and kept asking Dad for candy bars and beef jerkys and he kept saying yes. But as it got later and later, Ricky, Rosie and I started begging to go home.

"Yes, Frank, we've got to get these kids to bed," my mom said, running her long fingers over my hair, rubbing my back. She drank pop just like us. Dad was always hanging around the bar, with the players. And we were so tiny we had to go up behind him and pull at his striped softball pants and beg him to go home.

"Just one more, honey-doll," he'd say, and swing me up with his long arms to sit on the round plastic stool that said SCHMIDT BEER on it in white dirty letters. But that meant at least two or three more, so Mom dragged us out to the car, growing tense, saying to Dad as we passed his stool, "We'll be out in the car."

Dad's eyes looked funny, all bloodshot and lazy. He sat there on the stool, rolling green dice in a tan leather cup, gambling for free drinks. He still wore his softball spikes, the cleated soles crumbling with dried mud and grass from the field. His hair was messy and matted underneath the dark green softball cap, small black locks curling up around the edges.

In the long red station wagon, we waited patiently for Dad to come out. Every time I heard the squeak of the thin screen door, I looked, but it was someone else leaving, laughing and drunk. I hated seeing my mom then, quiet, her jaw muscles flinching tight.

"Lizzie, why don't you go in and try to get your dad to go home?" she asked me, not looking back, her voice thin and trembling.

I didn't want to, but climbed out of the car and jumped up the three cement steps into the hot smoky bar. The lighting was yellow-gold, like the light bulbs they hang out at county fairs and other outdoor night events. And there was Dad, one of the last customers in the place, his finger going round and round the rim of his beer glass—a thin white foamless layer left on the remaining beer.

"It's Lizzie!" he said as he turned around and saw me waiting, arms crossed, only three feet high in my bare feet and pink short set. But I didn't like him very much then. I wanted to get home to my big soft bed and go to sleep. My ponytails were falling out and getting tangled. I rubbed my eyes and yawned.

"I'll be right out. You tell your mom that, okay?" So I walked back to the car and told her that he'd be right out, and my mom just stared harder, only now she seemed desperate.

"Goddammit," she said through clenched teeth.

"What's the matter, Mom?" I asked her, but I knew. Rosie was always asleep, little head of blonde ponytails resting on the plastic seat. Ricky and I were more concerned about Mom, though. She never said very much, but if she did it was a swear word.

"Maybe you could just drive us home and Dad could find his own way back," suggested Ricky, but Mom just said, "Oh, Ricky, we'll get home."

And the next thing I woke up, wind whipping cold through the windows as we traveled down the highway home, my dad making all kinds of stupid talk with my mom. But she was crying and screaming at him, telling him he was a bastard, so irresponsible, what kind of a father was he, what a fine example he was setting for his kids . . . I pretended to be asleep.

SHOELACES

When I was in kindergarten, I didn't know how to tie my shoes. I went to school in Prospect, in the basement of a huge Catholic church, even though I was Lutheran. There we made pigeon soup, played house, and during Christmas, made papier-mâché bowls painted green and red for our parents. Mom dressed me in a calico dress, baggy red tights, and red corduroy tennis shoes. My legs were tiny noodles, thin and narrow under the nylon sags. She put ponytails in my baby-fine hair, leaving a crooked white part down the back of my head.

One day I went to school and found out we were having a test. We had to show the teacher that we could button buttons, count, say the alphabet, write our names and addresses, and tie our shoes. I was anxiety-stricken. No matter how hard I tried, I could not tie my shoelaces. Mom had been helping me for the past three weeks at home, but I could not do it.

"Lizzie, just concentrate," she said, "and watch Mom. See, it's not that hard." And with her long graceful fingers she would gently tie my dirty laces into a perfect bow.

"Mom, I can't."

"Sure you can. Now keep trying." Then she'd leave the room, leaving me on the floor with my frustrating shoelaces.

But Mom wasn't around and I had to tie them alone or everyone would think I was stupid, especially my teacher, Mrs. Watts.

"Lizzie, why don't you come over here and show me how you can tie your shoes," she said, and smiled with her coral-colored lips. "I'll be right back to see how you did." She smiled at me again.

Sitting on the blue carpeted square in the corner of the huge basement, I wanted to cry because I couldn't do it and everyone else could. I sat there and pretended. Then I saw June. She was a fat mentally retarded girl who had ruddy red cheeks and wore big swirly-print blue and green dresses with no waists. She knew how to tie her shoes, but it took her a long time.

"Julie," I whispered, leaning her direction, even though I was afraid of her. I thought mentally retarded people were dangerous. She was playing with the yellow hair of a doll in the kitchen center. Her tongue hung out, shiny with dribbles of saliva on it. Her blunt black hair hung in strings around her lemon-shaped face. "Julie," I whispered louder, "come over here once."

And she did. She smiled and threw the doll to the floor. She stomped over to me, her thick legs bulging under white tights and over the rim of her black patent shoes, like old ladies with fat feet packed into high heels. She squatted down next to me. I could see her pink-flowered underwear through her tights since her dress was hiked up around her stomach.

"What you want?" she asked, smiling. Her speech was slurred and slow. Her tiny eyes gazed dully into mine.

"I can't tie my shoes," I said very clearly, picking up the prop tennis shoe we had to use. It was a white rubber-toed sneaker with shiny silver eyelets. I set it in her red chubby hand. "Here, can you do it for me? Tie it?" I waited.

Her short fingers picked up the shoestrings as if they were tiny threads. She placed each one over the other, looking up at me after each move. As she concentrated harder, long clear strings of spit hung from her mouth. It kind of got to me, but at least she was helping me tie the stupid shoe.

"Can you kind of hurry up?" I asked her, growing nervous as more time passed. I sat on my knees and bounced. She looked at me and smiled again, laughing. "I make a flower," she said, snorting at the shoelaces looping around her fingers.

Then I heard the clicking of heels stop behind me. I smelled Mrs. Watts' sweet perfume mixed with Doublemint gum smell.

"Lizzie," she said sternly, "what's going on here? I wanted to see if *you* could tie your shoes, not Julie."

I looked down at the floor and started to cry. "I'm sorry, Mrs. Watts," I said. I could not look her in the eye. I could only see the black mist of her nylons covering her veiny legs.

"I think you should tell Julie you're sorry, too," she said, and put her arm around Julie.

"I'm sorry, Julie," I said, taking the knotted shoe out of her hands. She smiled and said something I couldn't understand, then galloped off to the kitchen counter, opening the cardboard mini-refrigerator and pulling out a tiny carton of plastic white eggs.

"Now let's see how *you* can tie your shoes," Mrs. Watts said. She pulled over a tiny pink chair from the reading table and sat next to me. She smoothed her gray skirt tightly over her thighs. She looked at her silver watch, then looked at me, smiling.

CRUEL

In third grade, Mrs. Rosen let us write on the chalkboard during free time, which excited us all a great deal. But that January, the cool girls ganged up on me and decided not to like me. This designated social outcast changed about every other month. I was a follower; I tried to fit in. I had one friend, Abby, who remained constant and loyal to me. She had long wavy blonde hair, but got it cut straight off at the neck one day. I had long straight brown hair, but cut it off at the neck in Abby's likeness.

One day we were all writing on the low, smooth blackboards and everyone started giggling. I looked up and saw that Wendy and Lynn and the cool girls had drawn a huge picture of me with ugly cutoff hair and a pig nose. It said DIZZY LIZZIE in big colored letters. Another picture showed me crying big triangle tears, sitting outside my trailer house. All day everyone called me Dizzy Lizzie and laughed. Even Abby laughed a little.

After math, we all got drinks at the water fountain, then went to the bathroom and waited in two single-file lines until everyone was finished. I was standing in line just minding my own business, when Tommy Kane, a new kid, ran up to me and pinched my nipple, hard. I didn't know what to do or where to look. He was a skinny, ugly kid with a lightbulb-shaped head. He had no friends; he was trying to fit in. All the boys hooted with laughter, shouting "Titty-twister Tommy!"

Mrs. Rosen said, "Shhh!" and glanced at her watch. Abby stood by me and told the boys to be quiet.

"They're just stupid boys," she said, "and besides, Wendy dared him to do it." Wendy was the leader of the cool girls who didn't like me that month.

"Why is Wendy so mean?" I asked as we walked back to our room.

"Maybe she's just jealous."

"Of what?" I wondered. I felt like nothing next to Wendy.

"I don't know," Abby said, sliding into her desk. "My mom said kids are just cruel."

THE 600

In fourth grade, we had to compete for the Physical Fitness Award in P.E. for a stupid patch and a certificate with the president's mimeographed signature. I hated it, even though I was the fastest girl in my class. Mr. Archer, our teacher, always made fun of me for trying to win the 600-yard dash.

"So, Lizzie, you gonna beat everyone again?" he said, laughing through his gritty yellowed teeth. He chewed on the metal whistle hanging over his gray pilled sweatshirt.

There was this girl Rita Bishop in my class who was pretty fast, too. We weren't really friends, but on the walk out to the track, I tried to talk to her.

"So, what was your time last year?" I asked.

"I don't remember."

"You want to run it together?"

"What?" she said wrinkling her nose at me. It was a red nose, pointy and shining in the sun.

"I mean, do you want to stay together and have a tie so neither of us has to win?" I was afraid she would beat me — she was pretty fast last year — so I thought I better play it safe. I had a title to uphold, and rather than surrender it, I thought I would share it.

"That's weird," she said, "because you always win." She was kicking a rock with her white and blue Nikes. I always wanted Nikes, but Mom said at the rate I was growing they were stupid. Besides that, I knew we could never afford them, so I had some plain white ones with thick waffle bottoms from Shopko.

"Well, do you want to?" I asked again.

"Okay," she said, "if it's such a big deal."

"It's not," I said, irritated, "but I just wanna."

Out at the track the boys waited on the inside circle of grass and laughed at the girls stretching out before the race.

"Lizzie will kick 'em all again," said Ed, my big, over-grown neighbor.

David gave me the thumbs-up Fonzie sign. All the girls gathered on the hot black track. You could actually see heat fumes rising up into the spring air. The black tar squished softly underneath my cushy tennies.

"On your mark, get set, go!" and Mr. Archer waved a little piece of green cloth.

As usual, I dashed out ahead of the whole pack, forget-ting about pacing and that I had a whole track and a half to run. Soon Rita was alongside me, red and pufflng, blonde hair bouncing with each step. We ran hard on the inside lane, smiling at the boys when we passed. They all thought I would win. My heart was growing huge and filling up my entire chest cavity. I wanted to be in the cool blue swim-ming pool at school, and splash and float. A quarter track to go—Rita right at my elbow. I felt like puking.

I saw the finish line. Mr. Archer stood there with his red stopwatch, all the boys huddled around the line in the grass.

Just then, right before the end, I pushed ahead with long reaching strides, crossing the line seconds before Rita. I ran to the edge of the track, then collapsed in the grass. I laid on my stomach, catching my breath as my lungs pushed against the earth. Two minutes flat. I was just six seconds under the fastest boy's time. But I had let Rita down. And what if she told everyone what I did?

Just then, Rita stood over me, sweating and limp. She had her hand on her hips, halfway doubled over with ex-haustion. She looked at me with squinted eyes, breathing heavily. "You're great, Lizzie. What a race." And she grabbed my hand and shook it real hard, letting it flop in my lap as she stalked away.

LOVERS

Carly was my favorite cousin to visit because she lived on a big farm in Iowa with barns and cows and pigeons and a dog, Snoopy, who always jumped up on me and licked my face. Carly was tough, a tomboy, and although I was two years older than her, she topped me in height and weight. I was delicate, from town, and so let her boss me around on the farm.

Carly's dad was really scary, even though he was principal of St. John's Lutheran Grade School. He was pick thin and tall with squinty eyes and a scaly red face. He always said I was his favorite niece, scanning me up and down with his little sawed-off yellow teeth grinning at me.

Once when I stayed overnight at their house, Carly and I were sleeping when suddenly we heard loud shouting downstairs. We ran down the bare wooden stairs in our flowered nightgowns, and watched as Carly's dad ran frantically from window to window in his blue terrycloth robe, pulling up the shades, then slamming them down. "Somebody's out there! Somebody's trying to get in!" he shouted. Then he ran to the glass gun cabinet and yanked out a rifle, ordering each of us to stand guard by a window. We stood frozen at our posts and listened intently, but only heard the sound of crickets and heat bugs. I was scared, and when he wasn't looking, grabbed Carly's hand and ran with her into her parents' bedroom, where her mom was sound asleep.

"Mom, Mom, wake up," Carly whispered. "It's Dad again." Her mother rolled over and wiped her eyes of sleep, then looked at the alarm clock.

"Oh, did he get you two out of bed? You shouldn't be up so late." She slipped on her robe and walked us back to Carly's room and tucked us both into the top bunk. "Don't mind Dad. There's no one out there."

The next morning I woke up late and knew Carly was already out in the barn, doing chores. I put on my cutoffs and a red halter top and ran outside to find her. The sun was hot and even the dry dirt was burning underneath my bare feet. I ran in long strides to the barn, stomping over large overgrown dandelion blooms on the way. The door was half-rotten; one side had worn away to form a handle. Carly had the milking machines pumping away at the lazy cows' teats. They stood there, oblivious, as the metal cylinders sucked away their milk. They seemed to enjoy it. Carly flicked the black switches on the wooden beam in the middle of the barn. Then she saw me.

"I was late getting up for chores and Dad's mad at me." She rolled her eyes, crossed her arms. She was big-boned and chubby, and self-consciously wore long pants and big shirts, even on hot summer days.

"Want to go back into the hay room now?" I asked. The cows would be busy milking for a while. Her eyes lit up and we snuck back to the corner of the barn, where tall rows of golden hay bales made walls of privacy. It smelled dusty and damp as we huddled down onto a bed of hay. "Are you going to be the man or me?" I asked her. Usually she was the man. Even though she was younger, she was still bigger.

"I'll be the man."

"You don't have to. I'll be it if you want."

"No, I'm being the man." I laid down on my back and she laid on top of me. Pulling off my red halter top, she tossed it by the strings onto the ground. She kissed my nipples, too hard, like she was biting them. I told her it hurt. So she rubbed her hands over them, gently.

We sat up, pulled off our shorts and underwear, then laid all our clothes on top of the hay bales. Carly rolled on top of me and rubbed her smooth body up and down against mine like we were making love.

"Harder?" she asked.

"Okay." Tiny pieces of itchy hay stuck to our backs and legs. Her thick body rocked down harder on mine. Carly put her finger into me and I felt it moving around. Meanwhile, the cows were still milking, their large teats sucked down to withered sacks. I thought I heard someone coming and jumped up, knocking Carly off balance. But it was nobody, just the pumping of the milking machines. We moved together in the August humidity, hair matted and skin wet with sweat. When Carly cupped her hand and placed it under my crotch, I laid there with my eyes wide open, looking at the thick spiderwebs laced between the wooden rafters overhead. She kissed my bellybutton and rubbed her face against my stomach. I hummed softly.

Suddenly all the milking machines went off in a slow whirl until it was completely silent. I blinked open my eyes and saw Carly's dad standing over us. His pinched face was enraged. We sat up and tried to cover ourselves.

"So," was all he said, unbuckling his belt. I looked at Carly, who looked away. Her dad stood before us in clean white briefs. I wanted to run away and go back to my mom, but he was too powerful, standing there in front of the door. Then he pulled his underwear off and dropped them in the crushed hay. I stared at the brownish purple penis hanging like a dead bird between his legs. I had never seen a man's penis before, only my little brother's small pink one. Carly's dad's was big and thick, with dark veins bulging out the sides. I looked at Carly, but she was looking her dad straight in the eye.

He walked over to close the rotting barn door. "Don't tell anybody about this," Carly whispered, turning her back to me.

He stalked back to us, brown penis poking up from his thin body like a stick. He stopped in front of Carly. Her big brown eyes filled with tears. "Now you be a good girl, Lizzie, and watch Carly." But I couldn't stay there and watch that long thing go into her. I felt like vomiting. I ran as fast as I could between the long row of cows who still had the metal tubes hanging limply off their pale teats. They snorted and glanced at me lazily as I bolted out the rotting door.

FEAR

Mom had Benjamin when I was eleven. Lots of hair, dark skin, like a papoose I could play mother with. As he grew, I took him for long walks in the stroller. I waved at all the cars that passed. I bought Lemonhead candies for Benjamin and poured them into the plastic tray in front of his little hands. He stuck pieces in his mouth until they were gummy and mushed, then spit them out in the tray where they hardened and collected flies.

One day I decided he was too big for the stroller, so I took him for a walk, carrying his diapered butt in my arms. As we were walking along the sidewalk of Main Street, the huge orange street cleaner came swooshing up beside us. Benjamin's small body clung tightly to me, his small fingernails scratching my skin.

"Git away!" he started to cry, which puzzled me, so I brought him home to play in his sandbox out by the grapevines.

Why was he so afraid of it? Whenever he saw its big stiff bristles scouring the street, Benjamin howled. When I saw it coming, I swept him up in my arms and ran to the road. Although he struggled and sobbed, I felt cruel and in control. I wanted to scare him.

One day Mom saw me carrying him to the road. Benjamin screamed and tried to hide in my chest at the sight of the street cleaner. I was relentless, until Mom came running out of the house. She held a damp dishtowel in her hand.

"Lizzie, what are you doing to him?" She grabbed Benjamin away. "You know he's scared to death of that thing. For god's sake, grow up already."

I stood there stupidly with my hands by my sides. Mom walked back to the house with Benjamin's legs dangling around her hips. His big brown eyes looked back at me as he hung on to Mom's soft shoulder. I watched as the big orange street cleaner continued moving down the street, blowing dust and leaves behind it.

SELFISH

One night I was up late reading *Teen* magazine and listening to the radio. I heard Rosie stir, and soon small feet padded up to the doorway of my room. She stood there with red sleepy cheeks and blonde tangled hair, rubbing her eyes.

"Lizzie, can I sleep with you?" she asked in a small groggy voice.

"Rosie," I said, "I hate it when you do this. Sleep in your own room."

"But I'm scared."

"If I let you sleep in my bed tonight, then you'll always want to. So, no."

She leaned her head against the doorway, waiting. I was getting really mad, because she had this way of making me feel guilty. Some nights I even heard her crying in her room.

"Okay," I said. "You can sleep on my floor. But only for tonight."

"Okay." She trotted off to her room to get her pillow and blankets, then arranged them in a cozy nest at the foot of my bed on the gray linoleum floor—the hard cold floor and it was winter. There I sat with big pillows propped up behind me, like some sort of queen, warm in my double bed that Rosie and I had slept in together for the first ten years of our lives, covered with the Raggedy Ann quilt our mom made for us. I almost told her she could sleep up with me just for tonight, but soon I heard her soft breathing, and I knew she was asleep. She had on my old flannel nightgown that was so worn you could barely see the tiny yellow flowers. The streetlights glowed in through the long lean windows that went almost to the floor, casting a soft peach light over Rosie's face. I could see the deep dimple in her chin. I used to call it her butt chin and she'd get mad, then laugh.

I thought about Christmas, how I always sang to her, "Christmas is coming, Rosie's getting fat, please put a penny in the old man's hat . . ." until she cried. Or the color snapshot of Rosie's fifth birthday party, where her face is red and blotchy from crying and Ricky and I are standing around her. She'd been picking at the white cake and I know we were teasing her about something, but I couldn't remember what.

There she was on my floor sleeping, because she was afraid. I thought again about waking her and letting her sleep up in the warm bed with me, where she would feel safe and press her body close to mine. I thought about it for a long time, but decided that life was hard, and that eventually everybody had to grow up, and eventually Rosie would know that, too.

TREATS

The bell tinkled as I opened the door of my grandparents' store—Eppler's Town and Country. They've run the store together forever, and I try to visit every Saturday and lend a hand. They've never hired outside help and they're darn proud of it, too. Everyone in Elwood loves and respects them, calls them Dorothy and Dick.

A rotten-fruity smell filled up my nostrils. Boxes of oranges, grapefruits, pears, grapes and green bananas lined the floor in front of the peanut butters and jellies. Yellowed cartoons clipped from newspapers decorated the old-fashioned cash register, ornate and tall.

"Hi Grandma," I said. We hugged over the low counter loaded with sausages and stacks of the thin local newspaper. Her delicate frame almost crushed under my grip, so I let go. She looked older, still doughy around the cheeks, but her mouth pulled taut into thin slits of dryness—a dusty pink. She put on her new glasses with the curving bows of gold, looking down through the glass at me, blinking.

I saw Grandpa's huge belly pushing at the middle of his pale green shirt, buttons strained and pearly white. "How we doin'?" he asked like he always did, leaning up against the long metal dispensers of Copenhagen and Skoal. The tiny bristles of his crewcut poked from his scalp like wires, half gray, half brown. His face was big and round and pink, like a baby's. I preferred Grandpa; Grandma scared me.

On Christmas and Easter, Grandma used to seek me out and put on her glasses, looking closely at all the pores on my face. Her hands were scratchy and flaky on my skin, the red pointed fingernails bringing layers of tears to my eyes as she bore down, forcing out the tiny blackheads.

"Ouch, Grandma, that hurts," I'd protest. She was relentless. She wouldn't let me go until she got them all out.

It seemed to give her satisfaction, poking down with the two glossy nails on my soft, preteen face, making deep red indentations — a subtle humiliation that left my face red and throbbing.

But in the store, they were king and queen. Grandma had the power to give or not give.

"Are you hungry? Get yourself something," she said.

I walked around the cramped wooden shelves, looking at Pop Tarts and sweetened cereal and sardines and the cheese that squirts out in a wavy line.

"Go ahead, you can have anything you want. Pick of the crop." Then she stood back and smiled.

It made me nervous, all the things I could have. Or not. I went back by the Lee overalls and jeans, feeling the blue stacks of crisp new denim. It smelled like a hot iron back there.

I thought about a twelve-pack of Pepsi, but at last took a package of those flat caramel circles to put around apples. Wrapples, they were called.

When I chose those, Grandma laughed. "That's what you're going to pick? Out of everything?" Her gold eyes flickered wildly behind the glasses. Her stained teeth ground back and forth, as if chewing on sand.

"Well, that's what I want," I said.

"Well, that's what you get," she said. Then she went back behind the counter by the candy bars and started blowing her nose, hard.

SIXTEEN

It was my sixteenth birthday and I wanted to kill myself. No one was around. I wandered around the house, hot and miserable. It was a humid day in the upper nineties and even my bra was damp. I went to the kitchen to pour myself a glass of grape Kool-Aid, but my heart ached. So I set the pitcher on the table and sat down on the sticky linoleum, leaning my face on the cool of the green refrigerator door. There was nothing else to do.

I got up slowly and walked to the window. Benjamin was running with his friends Timmy and Jason through the revolving spritz of the lawn sprinkler. They laughed as they stuck their little butts up close to the sprinkler, water pelting and running off their small swimming trunks.

I grabbed a family-sized bottle of Norwich aspirin off the kitchen windowsill. Shaking, I took a plastic tumbler out of the cupboard and left, letting the thin screen door slam behind me. I ran to the train trestle down at the edge of town, right behind the trailer court I used to live in.

Walking barefoot underneath the train tracks over the dusty hot red rock, my head pounded. I sat down by the water and ran my hands through my thin hair. The tar-smeared poles smelled bitter and nauseating. I matched the arrows of the aspirin lid and opened the bottle. Hundreds of powdery discs filled my hands. I dipped the tumbler into the thick hazy water with green and brown pieces floating in it.

I took the aspirins by threes until this became too tedious and slow. Finally, I dumped the contents into the dirty glass of creek water and chugged it down as if it was a glass of lemonade. Then they were gone. I tasted the bitter whiteness in my throat; the tart aspirin gagged me and made my eyes water. I laid down on the red rock, the sun pounding into me. I thought about death and God and if I would go to hell. I felt my stomach muscles churning the aspirin mixture around, swishing the disgusting potion with acids and juices. My ears were ringing loudly; I could hear nothing else. The creek continued to flow as I lay there, and a few crows flew overhead in a line.

I don't remember why, but I got up then. The world seemed to be turning fast. I laid down – it felt the same way. Finally I got up and tried to walk. I walked over the hot rocks, my feet covered with an orange powder. I was in a cold sweat. Suddenly I felt a deep surge of foam rising in my stomach. As if someone had turned a faucet completely open, the aspirin shot straight up my throat and splashed onto the red rocks. I looked at the fresh milky vomit shining in the sun. There was more, but it wouldn't come out yet. So I kept walking. I had failed.

Later that night in bed, I tried to fall asleep. My ears rang like piercing sirens, and I had both my blue pillows wadded over my ears and my hands were sore from pressing down so hard. The evening was cooler, but I was sweating in my bed, trying to rock myself to sleep. I heard Rosie's heavy breathing in the next room. My eyes wouldn't close. The white curtains that draped softly around my long windows sucked tightly against the screens, startling me. I ran downstairs to Mom and Dad's room, feeling my way down the dark stairway instinctively, like a bat.

Dad snored lightly. I stood and watched them, the fan billowing my short nightgown around me. What would I say? Then I sat down at the foot of their bed, the blue carpet sticky and rough on my bare skin. I laid on my stomach, hands over my ears, but the ringing wouldn't stop. I got up quietly, stood beside Mom and lightly touched her bare shoulder. She stirred instantly and asked what was going on.

"Mom I'm so sorry . . . I took a bunch of pills and I know it was . . . oh god, I'm sorry . . . but I feel so sick . . ."

Before I knew what was happening, Dad was on his feet. He threw the white sheets off himself, zipped into Lee cutoffs and looked for his glasses. I heard Mom calling the hospital. I stood there crying and holding my hands over my ears.

The nurses I knew, that's how small Prospect is. They stared at me, asked me questions.

"Honey, what did you take?"

"How do you feel now?"

"Did you vomit yet?"

Mom was crying and clutched her brown purse under her arm. She was smoking a cigarette and chewing gum. Dad was worse. His face was all blotchy and he was shaking, staring out the window, chain-smoking. He kept shaking his tired head and looking at everything in the room. Then he'd look down at the white floor and sniff his runny nose. I lay there as the nurses took off the tennis shoes that I had slipped on as we left the house. A small pile of sand and rocks fell out and sprinkled all over the fresh white sheets.

The nurse with gray-streaked hair and deep black eyes came in with a bedpan and some gray liquid I had to take to keep vomiting. It tasted like vanilla cement or that almond bark people put over tiny pretzels during Christmas. I lay on my side, gagging. Mom and Dad huddled over by the window, smoking cigarette after cigarette. They always had me run down to Tank 'n' Tummy just before it closed to get two packs of True Green 100's for Mom and two packs of Marlboros for Dad. The clerk had them on the counter when she saw me walk in the door. I hated getting them cigarettes.

The vomit-inducing medicine doubled me over with huge pushes from my stomach. I leaned over the bedpan and heaved up remnants of aspirin and saliva and pieces of leaves and grass from the dirty creek water.

Soon Mom and Dad came over to me, their eyes red and puffy. Mom had red splotches like amoebas all over her chest, which always happened when she was very upset or very hot. Dad looked at me with the saddest eyes I've ever seen, and then he looked down at his feet. His long legs were spindly and hairy standing there in his jean cutoffs. I had never noticed how thin he was.

"We're going to go now, so you can get some sleep. We'll be back early in the morning," he said.

"We love you," my mom said, kissing my sweaty forehead. It was the first time she ever said that to me.

They both looked old and tired standing there against all the whiteness. How I must be hurting them, I thought, but I couldn't say anything.

That night in the dark room I felt the IV pricking constantly into my vein, straining the thin skin that covered my hand. Neil Young was singing "Heart of Gold" on the small brown radio which sat on the hospital dresser. I wanted it off but was afraid to get up. My head still hummed in a fuzz. The nurses shuffled in and out of my room to check on me, bringing me apple juice, grape juice, orange juice in tiny plastic cups to flush out my system.

The sheets were cool and tight over my bare legs. I heard the nurses talk about their kids at the front desk, and then a tiny baby cried, muffled by glass walls. I lay flat on my back and closed my eyes. I wanted to be dead.

THE LAWNMOWER

Dad saw the sign about a mile away. LAWNMOWER THIS WAY it said in black paint, attached to a stick shoved in the ditch. He and Mom had just picked me up from college in the rusting red Toyota to take me home for a weekend. We pulled into the short gravel driveway. Chickens scampered off near the farmhouse.

In the small brown yard lawnmowers stood diagonally in a row. Their homemade red price tags blew in the wind. Over by the weathered shed stood an old milk-white icebox with blue trim, big metal bars for handles. It was almost tipped over in the soft green grass.

Dad yanked the emergency brake so we wouldn't roll away, and got out of the car. I saw him feel the butt of his jeans for his wallet.

"Your dad," Mom sighed. "He thinks he has to hit every sale from here to Minneapolis." She leaned back in the black vinyl seat and lit up a cigarette.

Dad was out inspecting the grease-covered mowers, while the old man in overalls ignored him. There were half a dozen lawnmowers, and Dad pushed around every one, tipping them over to see the sharpness of the thick metal blades underneath. He looked over at the car and waved to us, smiling proudly with one hand on the mower. He pretended to mow the lawn, then laughed. Mom and I laughed.

I used to hate the fact that we never had any money and shopped at thrift stores and got free lunch tickets and that our cars were always secondhand without mufflers or brakes or with cracked windshields. Dad would laugh at my distress and say, "Lizzie, you have to start your own style. Do your own thing." Then he'd tell the story I'd already heard about him and his friend Bill being the first ones in Prospect to start the Bermuda shorts trend.

"No one ever wore them until Bill and I showed up one night wearing plaid Bermudas. Of course, they all laughed at first, but the next week, everyone was wearing them."

I could tell he must have been wild in his youth. He got kicked off the baseball team his junior year for smoking, and according to him, if he hadn't, scouts from the pro leagues were checking him out, and he could've made it professionally. That was the story of his life . . . if only this, if only that.

I used to think that by the time I grew up and went to college, he'd start making good money somehow, but it never happened. It used to seem so important when I lived there, to be like every other family. I don't know what happened, but I learned how hard it is to get money. I learned fast about bills and eating canned soup seven days a week and paying insurance and what really makes people happy.

When I went home for Christmas last year, we went to the secondhand store in Prospect to look for an old leather coat. Years ago, I would've sunk down in the seat with embarrassment, driving down Main Street with my dad in a rattling green station wagon, pulling into a thrift store. But it was okay. It didn't matter.

And as I watched him finger the price tags of the old lawnmowers, I appreciated his way of living. Slowly. Easily. Enjoyably. Mom told me he had a new job in a machine shop as a supervisor. She got so frustrated between jobs, going up to the post office twice a day, looking for that unemployment check, coming home bitter and depressed.

"They don't seem to realize that we have to put food on the table for these kids," she would shout at my dad, who silently smoked a Marlboro. "And you don't even give a shit!" she'd say and start crying. Dad would tell her to relax, everything would work out.

I watched Dad wheel an orange lawnmower over to the chubby farmer in striped worn overalls. He pulled out his wallet and handed the farmer a few bills, which the farmer deposited promptly in the pocket of his chambray shirt.

"I wonder how much he had to pay for that?" I said to Mom, who was snapping her Big Red gum.

"Oh god, who knows," she said. "At least he'll mow the lawn now."

"That's true." Then Dad came back with his greasy mower, beaming. He shoved it in the hatch of the car.

A few chickens fluttered and clucked as the Toyota jerked out of the narrow gravel driveway, back onto the smooth pavement.

PEACH WINE

I came home for Christmas and walked across the alley to
visit my grandparents. They're retired, but Grandpa still
talks about the creamery they used to own and sometimes
we watch the home movies of the big machines folding soft
yellow butter in silver tanks. Now Grandpa reads *National
Geographic* and Grandma prays all the time.

This time, Grandma had a sick headache and the whole
room smelled like Ben Gay. She lifted her head from the
couch. "Do you want some wine, Lizzie?" I was stunned.
She never drank, and after about forty years of marriage,
still got upset when Grandpa had a bottle of Blatz.

"Sure, I'll have a small glass." Grandma padded into the
kitchen and I heard glasses clinking.

"She's just drinking that because she had some at
Pastor's the other night," Grandpa whispered. He wore
tan corduroys and a flannel shirt. He was completely bald.

"Here you are, Lizzie," Grandma said, handing me a
long-stemmed goblet of amber wine. *Fiddler on the Roof* was
on the tv. I noticed their tree wasn't up yet.

"Grandma, where's your tree?" I asked. She usually had
it up the day after Thanksgiving.

"Oh, you know us old folks. We had to get an artificial
this year. Grandpa's getting too old to haul a big tree in
every year. Isn't this wine good? It's peach — peach wine.
Pastor gave me a little nip the other night."

Grandma had become very religious. If I didn't go to
church on Sundays, she wouldn't speak to me for the entire
day. Usually she caught our whole family still in pajamas
at noon, drinking coffee, the Sunday paper spread all over
the floor.

My grandparents practically raised us when Dad was
drinking so much and Mom worked. After school we went

over to their big house and watched sitcom after sitcom until "The Brady Bunch," when Mom came to pick us up. Grandma had the greatest candy jar, which we'd always try and dip into, only it was right by Grandpa's chair. He would nap for a while, then we'd tiptoe up to the end table, gently lifting the orange crystal lid of the jar, feeling for the squareness of a caramel or the bumpy oblongness of root beer barrels.

Grandma looked funny in her new sweatsuit. She had a little wad of Kleenex stuck between her belly and the stretch waistband. She hacked up phlegm and folded it up in her Kleenex wad. "Doctor says you have to throw it out," she said. She sat with her legs folded underneath her, wrapped in an afghan of earth tones. She tapped her foot as she talked, and rocked her body slightly.

"Do you think I should have your mother give me a permanent?" she asked, fingering her short gray hair. She lost the aged auburn color of her hair after chemotherapy a few years back—cancer of the uterus—and now her hair was a soft white shag.

"Oh, no, I really like it this way," I said to her, nodding my head and meaning it. She finally had her color back and looked healthy. She wore pointed yellow tennies, and pale peach polish shone on her nails. She pulled out a Sears sale catalogue and opened to a page of ladies blazers.

"What do you think of this here?" she asked, pointing her long fingers at a woman wearing a camel-colored wool blazer. "I thought it would be nice for church, and it would go with all my plaid skirts. Do you like it?"

"I do," I said, "a lot." She had simple taste, very classic and neutral. Just like her hands—very long, well-manicured fingers, nail polish only in the most basic shades. When she and I and my mother sat around her kitchen table drinking tea and talking, we would always cluster our three generations of hands in the middle of the table, marveling at the striking similarities. Mine were a little more gnawed than theirs, Mom's were rough and puffy, and Grandma's were oily and shiny from lotion. Gold rings turned loosely around her fingers.

"So tell me about school," she said and I did, boiling hot water for tea, knowing she wouldn't give me more wine.

The English coffee house of the 1600s
was a place of fellowship where
ideas were freely exchanged.

The Parisian cafes of the early 1900s
witnessed the birth of dadaism,
cubism and surrealism.

The American coffee house of the 1950s,
a refuge from conformity for beat poets,
exploded with literary energy.

This spirit lives on in the pages
of Coffee House Press books.

The Price of Eggs was designed by Allan Kornblum using the Xerox Ventura desktop publishing system. The Palacio type was generated by Stanton Publication Services; the Lydian display type was set in metal at Coffee House Press. Coffee House Press books are printed on acid-free paper and have sewn bindings for durability.